A Time for Angels

A Time for Angels

Making and Giving Away Angels
at Christmastime Sets Love in Motion
for Two Couples

SANDRA PETIT AND GAIL SATTLER

BARBOUR
PUBLISHING

Angel on the Doorstep

Sandra Petit

Dedication

I'd like to dedicate this story to
crocheters across the globe.
A special thank-you to those who helped with
Moira's angel pattern, as well as those who
sent me encouragement through
my crochet Web site (www.crochetcabana.com).
You can find more detailed instructions
on Moira's angel (with pictures) at
www.sandrapetit.com. Enjoy!

Chapter 1

Moira Sullivan patted the shiny red heart sequin onto the angel just as the chimes of the doorbell sounded. Working swiftly, she gathered the rest of the crocheted angels from the end table, hurried to the rolltop desk, and threw all the angels inside, firmly pushing the top down to hide them.

The doorbell rang again, causing her to quicken her pace to the entryway. She ran her fingers through her hair, patted it down, and took a deep breath before opening the door.

"Mr. Corrigan." Moira stood with the door open, finding herself lost in the way the sun highlighted his midnight black hair and deepened his blue eyes.

Tall, dark, and handsome. The old cliché fit Joe Corrigan perfectly.

He nodded at her slowly. "Please call me Joe. After all, we're part of the same church family." He stood quietly, hands in his pockets.

"And I'm Moira." Yes, they were part of the same church family, but that family was huge and she barely knew him. She suddenly realized she was keeping him waiting in the cold air. She felt the heat of a blush move up her neck. "Oh, I'm sorry. Come on in." She backed away, allowing Joe to move past her into the foyer. "The angel is in the living room. I'll get it."

Instead of remaining in the foyer as she had hoped, Joe followed, chatting as they walked. Moira glanced at Snowflake, her French poodle, hoping the dog might provide some distraction. Instead, he simply lifted his head to give Joe a cursory glance, then lowered his muzzle to rest on his paws and closed his eyes. *Some help you are.*

"It's nice of you to return the angel to Mother. After all, you paid for the desk at the yard sale as is. Mother was so embarrassed when she realized she'd left her angel inside."

"It's not a problem. The angel is hers. It would be wrong to keep it."

Moira stopped at the end table where she had placed Anna Corrigan's angel. It wasn't there. With dismay, she realized she must have put it in the desk with the others. She bit her lip. There was nothing to do but open the desktop and retrieve Anna's angel. That was why Joe was here.

"I was just looking at the angel, and I must have put it in the desk without thinking," she mumbled as she moved toward her newly purchased rolltop desk. *Stay by the sofa*, she mentally commanded Joe. But unfortunately, Joe once again followed her.

"How is that working out? Do you like the desk? Have any trouble with the rolltop? It used to stick sometimes for Mother."

"It's working out fine. The top isn't too much trouble. I just need to jiggle the knobs a bit to open it. Otherwise, I love the desk. It was a terrific find."

Moira took hold of the round wooden knobs and tried to lift the top, but it wouldn't budge. She shifted her weight and wiggled the knob again. *Now? You have to stick now?* She pressed down while lifting, hoping to dislodge it. Without warning, the top flew open. Angels catapulted everywhere. Out of the corner of her eye, she saw Joe's eyes widen. She refused to look at him while they both bent to gather the angels.

"Hey, I know this angel." Joe stood, examining her creative handiwork.

"Oh no," she mumbled, then cleared her throat, stiffened, and walked toward him. "Thank you," she said curtly, reaching to snatch the familiar angel—though not his mother's—from Joe's hand.

Joe moved his hand away, lifting the angel higher so she couldn't reach it. Her five-foot frame was no match for Joe's six-foot frame. Growling, she jumped up. "Joseph Corrigan, please give me that angel!" She felt like a schoolgirl trying to get a favored toy.

"Only my mother calls me Joseph, and of course I'll give it to you. In a second." His gaze moved upward as he inspected the white crocheted angel, obviously noting the distinctive red heart-shaped sequin.

Moira's stomach churned while Joe turned the angel over and over. Joe Corrigan wasn't stupid. She didn't want him to recognize her specially made angel, but she didn't think Joe was the type to let something go until he was good and ready to do so.

Moira crossed her arms, tapped her foot as loudly as she could, and waited.

"My friend Manny Wiseman has one just like this. It appeared on his desk at the real estate office." Joe's brow crinkled, and he frowned. "Manny told me another one of the deacons also received one just like his. And Pastor John. . ." His eyes widened. "You're the undercover angel!"

Moira blinked. "The what?"

"Undercover angel. That's what they're calling her —*you*. The angels appear out of nowhere, in the oddest places, when the person least expects it, and no one knows who's doing it. You know, like an undercover agent." He paused, and his voice became more solemn. "Manny was having a terrible week. He'd gotten some bad news about his health. He went to lunch, and when he returned, there was the angel sitting on his desk. It made his day."

Moira smiled, glad the timing for *that* delivery had been good, if coincidental. "What makes you think I'm this 'undercover angel' person?" she asked, despite the evidence of angels strewn about her feet. "Maybe I'm holding the angels for the real undercover angel. After all, she wouldn't want to be caught with all these angels on hand. Or maybe I got one and decided to make more." She knew she was rambling, but she was running out of explanations for the angels' presence in her home.

Joe rolled his eyes and shook his head. "Nice try, but it looks like they're only going to the Faith Church staff. You're not on the staff. What kind of work do you do anyway?"

Moira's shoulders slumped. She was busted. "I'm a crochet designer. I write crochet books."

Joe's deep voice erupted in a hearty laugh. "Aha! Had I known that, I would have figured it out. Mother never mentioned it."

"She probably doesn't know. I've only just started making enough to do it full time, and I only spoke to your mother briefly at the sale." She sighed. "Joe, you can't tell anyone. It's supposed to be anonymous."

She didn't like the gleam that appeared in his eyes. "Anonymous, huh? Why?"

"Well. . ." *Why indeed?* How was she going to explain this? She took a deep breath. "I just want to show the staff I appreciate them. I don't want credit. It won't mean as much if they know."

"So it's important to you that it *remain* a secret."

"Yes. *Very* important." She stressed *very*, hoping it would make a difference.

Joe quirked one eyebrow, and a corner of his mouth curled up. Moira's heart pounded as she watched him slowly turn the angel over in his hands, inspecting it again.

"Do you think one of these will appear on Gabe's doorstep?"

Moira's heart began to beat faster. "Gabe?"

"Yes. He's the older gentleman who always sits in the back corner. Did you know that once a month, during the week, when no one is there except the pastor, he comes in and washes the dirt and bird droppings off the cross outside?"

"He does?"

"Yeah. Once you get to know him, he's a funny old guy. He doesn't want anyone to know what he's doing. But I know. And I think he should get one of these."

Moira mentally added Gabe to her list of angel recipients.

"I'll give him one, too. What's his address?"

He grinned widely. "If you really want to know, then I guess you'd better cut me in on the action."

"There's nothing to cut you in on," Moira said slowly. "I'm not making any money. In fact, it's costing me materials and time."

"Then there's even more reason to cut me in. I can't make the angels, obviously, but I can help with the expense. And I can help you deliver them. Maybe together we can think of interesting places to stash the angels. You know, sort of keep it mysterious."

"I've been doing fine on my own." She plucked

the angel from Joe's hands.

"But you could do so much better with my help."

Moira tilted her head, thinking. This was her idea. She'd made the angels, and she'd already delivered several with no problem. She didn't need Joe's help, despite what he thought. Immediately her conscience chided her. Did she want the credit after all? The mere idea made her squirm. There was nothing wrong with letting someone else help. Joe appreciated the church staff, too. Maybe he just wanted to show his appreciation. *Practice what you preach, Moira.*

On the other hand, Joe wasn't a small person. The phrase "bull in a china shop" came to mind. Slipping in and out without getting caught would be a challenge, but it might also put more fun into her self-appointed job. And what if they *were* caught? While it wouldn't be such a big thing, she did want to do this anonymously.

Yet she doubted Joe would give her much choice. Would he really tell everyone what she was doing? Perhaps out of some misguided sense of fair play. Or maybe just because he could. Though she'd seen Joe at Faith Church for years, they were little more than acquaintances, and she wasn't sure what he would do.

She had no choice. She had to include Joe.

Having made the decision, she was surprised to find the idea wasn't totally repulsive to her. In fact, sharing a secret with Joe might be. . .fun.

"All right, you can help, but you can't tell a soul."

He frowned. "Not even my mother?"

She hesitated. Already the circle of those who knew was expanding. "Can your mother keep a secret?"

This time Joe hesitated. "Well, she does like to talk. Evidenced by our phone bill."

"You live with your mother?"

Joe bristled. "Yes. She's been alone since Dad died, except for me."

Moira quickly backpedaled. "I didn't mean anything by it. Sorry if I hit a nerve. I guess it surprised me because my own parents don't live around here. In fact, they live in separate states."

Joe's shoulders slumped as he sighed. "That's okay. I overreacted. It's just that people always look at me funny when they first find out. They expect a thirty-four-year-old man to be on his own. Really, I *am* on my own. I'm an attorney, and I pay all the bills and cover all the expenses."

Attorney. The word leaped out at her. Moira opened her mouth to speak, but no words came out. She finally forced herself to take a breath and speak

15

calmly. "You're a lawyer?"

"Yes, I'm a defense attorney. I could have moved Mother to my place when she began to have health problems, but she's comfortable in her own home, so I chose to move in with her."

Moira nodded slowly. "It's very nice of you to care for her." It was nice, especially for a man who made his living helping criminals go free so they didn't have to pay for their crimes, regardless of the horrible things they had done. How did a Christian man reconcile that kind of thing with his faith—being a part of the process that allowed the guilty to go free, using whatever technicality and loophole in the law he could find?

Joe's voice was hardly above a whisper as he shrugged his shoulders. "Honor our parents. It's what God tells us to do." Then he straightened and rubbed his hands together, lifting his voice. "So what do we do first?"

Honor your parents, but otherwise manipulate the truth when it suits your purposes. Already she regretted her agreement, but she wouldn't go back on her word. She had no choice in the matter. "We make a list."

Chapter 2

Joe lifted his finger from the doorbell just as the door swung open. Moira reached out to grab his arm, pulling him inside.

"I need you to put these angels together," she said as she dropped her hold of his arm and hurried into the living room, apparently assuming he would follow, which he did.

Joe's gaze moved over the room, where pieces of angels were scattered on every conceivable surface in organized groups. He'd only seen completed angels when he was here last week. Moira's poodle, Snowflake, lay paw over paw, asleep in a corner.

"What?"

Moira turned and pointed to the table in front of the sofa. "I'm almost finished with this group, but there are enough full angels finished for you to start putting them together. The glue gun is hot."

Joe extended his arm to encompass the mass of angels scattered about.

"Moira, what are you talking about?"

She frowned as though it were him who wasn't making any sense when he had no clue as to what she meant. Joe noted the dark circles under her eyes and the harried expression on her face.

"I've made a good start on the additional angels—"

He raised his hand, palm toward her. "Stop. What angels?"

Moira sighed. "Before I started delivering, I made enough angels for the church staff, deacons, and Sunday school teachers. I hadn't thought of all the folks you mentioned, those who work behind the scenes, who don't get any recognition. The ones on the list we made when you picked up your mom's angel. I've stayed up late every night this week so we'd have enough angels to go around. I don't want anyone left out. Since I made all the parts separately, the process went faster. The wings take longest because they're all single crochet, so I'm not quite finished." She paused and glared at him. "Is there a problem here? I thought you wanted to help."

Moira's expression told him she was more than a little annoyed, but Joe had a feeling she was just tired and it was her fatigue that was causing her irritability.

"Sure I want to help, but I thought I would be delivering, not making. I'm not sure I understand what you want me to do. I certainly don't know how to crochet."

She shook her head, and a small frown appeared, causing the sides of her eyes to wrinkle. He thought it was the cutest thing he'd ever seen, even though her ire was directed at him.

"I know that. You don't have to crochet. All you have to do is glue the pieces together with the hot glue gun. I'll show you. It's really easy, and it will give me time to finish. I'm making a few extra in case we think of more people who should get one."

Joe stared at the pieces. Glue. He could handle glue. His confidence kicked up a notch.

Yet, while it was a good sign that she was asking for his help, he wasn't sure what his status was after he'd blackmailed her into accepting that help. For now, it seemed she had honestly accepted it. He was a part of this project. Now she was handing him the opportunity to show her he was serious.

"Okay, show me what to do."

Moira demonstrated how to attach the head,

wings, and red heart sequin to the body. He'd never seen such a small glue gun in his life. It certainly wasn't like his big, old, black, standard model at home. He felt awkward handling Moira's miniature version with his large hands, and squeezing just the right amount of the sticky substance without making a mess was a little more difficult than he'd expected, but not so hard he couldn't do it.

"This is certainly different," he commented. He could attest that it wasn't anything like his day job, standing in a courtroom trying to convince judge and jury of the innocence of his clients.

"Different?"

"I spend most of my time in a courtroom, though I think some of my clients may have had their own personal angels helping out."

When he glanced over at Moira, he noticed her stiffen and wondered what he'd said to cause the reaction.

"Have you ever been in a courtroom?"

"Yes." The word fell from her mouth reluctantly.

Yes? Joe couldn't help frowning. When Moira didn't elaborate, he began to wonder if there was a reason the two of them had never seen one another socially. Moira didn't look like a criminal, but over the years he'd come to realize there was no particular look for a person in that position. They came in all shapes and sizes. Should he pursue the subject or wait until she felt comfortable enough to share? There were other reasons, besides being a criminal, that a person could enter a courtroom. Maybe she'd had a speeding ticket, or perhaps she'd sat on a jury.

Moira took up her crocheting, and Joe resumed his job of gluing the angel faces onto the bodies and then joining the pieces to the wings. While he worked, he took every opportunity to sneak a glance at Moira, trying to figure out what she was thinking. Her thick auburn hair fell into her face as she concentrated on her work. She seemed more relaxed as she crocheted. Maybe now that she saw everything would be done, she would be able to slow down and enjoy the process.

Joe glanced down and realized he had glued a wing on upside down.

"Uh, Moira?"

Moira lifted her head to look in his direction. "Yes?"

"I think I may have messed up this one."

He didn't know what he'd expected, but Moira didn't react. She rose from the couch and walked over to examine what he'd done.

"It's upside down. Not a big problem since it's basically the same top and bottom, but it's better if the chenille stem is on top. It's not hard to fix. We just have to reheat the glue, pull the two pieces apart, and reglue them correctly."

Joe was relieved to note Moira's smile. "Right. . .but won't hot glue come out if I use this gun?"

"Yes, but we won't use that one. I have a separate gun, with no glue stick inside, for situations like this."

Joe grinned. "You've done this before?"

"Sure. Everyone makes mistakes sometimes."

Her face was unreadable, but her body stiffened when he leaned over to watch her work. Joe backed up, giving her space. He wondered if there was a hidden meaning in her statement.

Picking up the angel, Moira showed him how to correct the problem. He was determined he wouldn't need to know, however, because he wasn't going to make the mistake again. He knew each individual angel took about an hour to crochet. Moira had worked hard, and he didn't want to be the one who caused her more trouble.

After she'd repaired his angel, Moira showed him how to cut the Styrofoam cones and pack everything for delivery.

"What are the white cones for?" he asked.

"You put the angel on top of the cone so it will stand upright. I could have starched them, but sometimes people store their Christmas things in the attic, and some pests are attracted by the starch," Moira explained.

Joe nodded. "These little notes are a nice touch." He held up the small card with a note thanking the recipient, Elizabeth Wright, for her service as church organist.

Moira looked up. "I was afraid they might be too much."

"I don't think so. The sentiment is real, and I know the recipients will appreciate it."

She smiled, but the smile didn't reach her eyes; and Joe wondered if he'd done anything to make her feel uncomfortable in his presence. Thinking back, he thought he'd been the perfect gentleman, but they *were* alone in her home. Maybe that was all it was.

He watched her return to her spot on the sofa where she continued working on the remaining wings. Her nose crinkled as she yawned, and he noticed her fingers, though nimble, moved more slowly. As he watched, they slowed even more, and then her hand stopped moving and he heard a soft sigh. His gaze shifted, and he saw her fatigue had gotten the better of her.

He finished gluing together the last angel, then walked to the sofa.

"All done."

Moira started and lifted her head. "What? Oh, you're finished already?"

"Yes. You can check them later, but I need to get going now. Maybe we could meet Friday evening to deliver some of these?"

"Okay." Moira put down her work and stood to walk him to the door. Even that simple action seemed to take great effort.

"I can find my way out. Why don't you catch up on some of that sleep you lost? I'll see you tomorrow."

He walked to the door, hoping she would return to her seat, but Moira followed him and gave a brief wave as he put his SUV into gear and moved off. Thoughts of Moira's smile occupied his mind as he made his way home.

Chapter 3

Sitting in the passenger seat of Joe's SUV, Moira glanced at Joe, who sat behind the wheel ready to drive to the home of tonight's undercover angel assignment. They'd spent several previous nights delivering angels. While Joe's ideas were innovative and he had helped her think of many who deserved an angel, it seemed something went wrong with almost every delivery. The recipients were still in the dark about where the gifts came from, but Moira was mentally exhausted at the end of the evening. She was determined not to let the mishaps get to her, however. The angels were delivered, and that was the important thing.

"Who's first on the list tonight?" Joe asked.

"I thought we could go by Jake Simon's house

first. He leaves his car unlocked, and he and his wife retire early. We can leave one in his car."

"Jake the groundskeeper?"

"Yes," Moira replied, buckling her seat belt as they prepared to leave.

"Why does he leave his car unlocked?"

"He's hoping someone will steal it," Moira said in all seriousness. "I heard him tell Mrs. Franklin that his wife won't let him sell it."

"Really? If I remember right, that was one of the last Volkswagens off the assembly line, just before the plant stopped production."

"That was a long time ago, wasn't it?" Moira asked the question not so much because she was really interested in old cars, but to stave off an awkward silence as Joe started the car and drove toward Jake's residence.

"Late seventies."

"Wow. And it still runs?"

"It runs fairly well. Jake's an amateur mechanic, so he's able to keep it going. Guess he'd like to put it out to pasture and get something newer."

"Apparently Mrs. Simon disagrees with that philosophy." Moira wrinkled her nose and tucked her hair behind her ears.

As they turned onto Jake's street, Moira pointed to an empty spot at the end of the block, a short distance from a streetlight. "Stop over there. We don't want to park too close."

Joe turned his head and lifted his brows at her command.

Moira squirmed under his gaze. "I just meant that Jake might look out the window, and it would be suspicious if there was another vehicle in his driveway."

"Got it." Joe pulled to a stop at the indicated spot, a short distance from Jake's house, opened his door, and slid from behind the wheel.

Deciding to leave well enough alone, Moira twisted to reach between the bucket seats to the back of the vehicle. The angels sat in a cardboard box, covered with a piece of black felt; so if anyone looked in, they wouldn't be able to determine what the box held. Careful not to flatten it, she retrieved Jake's angel, which had a little card attached with Jake's name and a note of thanks. As she turned back to face the front, the passenger door opened and Joe stood outside, his hand out to help her exit.

Moira's breath caught. She couldn't remember the last time a man had opened any door for her, much less walked around a vehicle to go to the trouble. On their previous deliveries, she hadn't given him time to show this side of his personality. She'd hopped right out as soon as they arrived at their destination. She wished Joe wasn't acting like such a gentleman. He was a lawyer. Just like her dad. Not just any lawyer, but a criminal lawyer. He kept felons out of jail. She resolved not to allow herself to think of Joe as anything other than the person who'd blackmailed her into helping with this project.

Joe extended his hand, and she had no choice but to grasp it or look churlish. He pulled to help her out of the vehicle, since her other hand held the angel.

Once Moira exited the car, Joe released her hand and led the way toward Jake's house.

They had gone only a few steps when a bark sounded somewhere behind them. Moira turned her head to see a large dog coming up behind them.

"Joe?"

"Yeah?"

"There's a dog following us."

Joe glanced behind them. "Pretty big dog, too."

"Maybe he smells cat on me. I was at my friend Elizabeth's earlier, and she has cats."

"Possibly, but he's a bit far for that, I think. I can't tell what kind of dog it is in this light. I can just tell that it's big. Keep walking."

Moira didn't want Joe to think she was afraid, but she picked up the pace anyway. Joe stayed right with her. Keeping close, he moved his hand to her bent elbow. She resisted the urge to shake it off, because she had a feeling it would be smart to stay close to Joe as long as they were being followed by Attila. Unfortunately, the dog also began to walk faster, and the distance between them became less with every step.

"He's still following us," she whispered.

In sync, the two of them walked even faster. The dog's growl was uncomfortably close behind them.

"Joe, he's coming after us!" Moira forgot all she knew about dogs and began to run.

Joe easily ran in place beside her but stayed close. Moira was grateful, because she knew he could have easily outdistanced her and left her to be mauled by the animal.

"I hope you're right about Jake keeping his car unlocked!" Joe yelled.

Moira realized they were in Jake's driveway, coming up to Jake's faded red Volkswagen. Safety was only a few steps away.

Suddenly Moira turned her head to look back, instinct telling her the dog was close. Then everything happened at once. With a loud bark, the large, black dog, which she now saw was a Doberman, rushed toward them. Joe swung open the Volkswagen door, yelled at Moira to get in, and shoved her to be sure she obeyed immediately.

Without worrying about propriety, and wanting to make room for Joe, Moira scrambled past the steering wheel and over the stick shift, landing on her knees on the passenger seat. Caught in an awkward position in limited space, she struggled to turn around to a proper sitting position as Joe slid behind the steering wheel, his knees hitting the dash. The door closed as the dog hit it.

Moira's breath caught at the sight of flashing fangs as the canine tried to get at them. Its sharp bark was ferocious and so loud that it hurt her ears. For a long moment neither of them said anything.

"You have a dog. What should we do?" Joe asked.

Moira shook her head. "I have a poodle. It's not exactly the same thing."

"I wonder whose dog it is." Joe's calm statement triggered her feelings of guilt. After all her talk of being prepared, here they were stuck in a Volkswagen, about to become dog food.

Moira leaned in his direction to try to look out

the window at the dog, which had stopped jumping against the door. She hoped Jake's car wasn't scratched. She craned her neck to get a better glimpse of the animal. Maybe it wasn't as big as she'd first thought.

No. It was big all right. She hadn't exaggerated, even in her thoughts. "I don't know, but it certainly would have helped to know about Attila in advance. I'm sorry." She sighed.

Joe chuckled. Moira's eyes widened. She didn't see anything funny about their situation.

"Why are you sorry? You didn't ask him to chase us into the car. Probably a neighborhood dog that got loose by accident. I've seen it happen a lot. We can call animal control—when we can get to a phone—and they'll pick it up."

"I guess you're right. But now what do we do?"

"I guess all we can do is wait. Maybe Jake will hear the commotion and come out."

Moira had little hope of that, knowing the elderly Jake and his wife were both hard of hearing—not that she wanted Jake to hear anything. That would ruin the surprise. "Listen. He's not making any commotion. He's just sitting there, watching us. And even if Jake does come out, what would we say? If he sees the angel, he'll know why we're here."

Joe's gaze also turned toward the window.

"Wonder how long he intends to stay there," she mumbled.

"Until something else catches his interest and pulls him away."

The dog sat on its haunches, his gaze glued to the door they had disappeared behind. Did the dog realize they were trapped? She knew guard dogs were trained to act just this way, but if this were a guard dog, nothing was going to pull him away.

Forty minutes later, they were still in the car and the dog was lying beside it, seeming to sleep, though they suspected it was just waiting.

"We can't stay here all night," Joe said.

Moira lifted her hand to move her hair behind her ears but stopped herself just in time. She knew it was a nervous habit, and there was no reason to let Joe know how jittery she was. "I know that."

"Why don't we just blow the horn? Jake will come out and chase the dog away, or at least call someone."

"Jake probably wouldn't hear it, and it would just get the dog barking again. Besides, I don't want him to know we're here. You know how important it is to me for this to be a secret."

"More important than sleeping in your own bed tonight?"

Moira glared at Joe. "Yes. No. Oh, you're impossible."

"Me? Do you want to spend the night in a Volkswagen?"

"Of course not. Don't you have a cell phone?"

"Don't you?" he countered.

"Yes, but it's in my purse. In *your* car."

"Good planning," he mumbled as he sank down into the seat, then crossed his arms over his chest. "It's not a car. It's an SUV."

Moira gritted her teeth. "Whatever." She'd been delivering angels for over a month before Joe was added to the team, and she had never had this kind of problem.

"Look. He's moving."

At Joe's words, Moira turned and stared at the offending animal. He was indeed moving—in the direction of a white cat that had entered his territory.

Run, cat, run.

"Come on. We can get out of here while the dog is distracted chasing the cat."

"He'll see us."

"We'll be quiet."

He didn't wait for Moira's okay but opened the door.

"Wait. The angel." Moira quickly set the angel

on the dashboard and, as quietly as she could, exited through the passenger door.

The trot back to Joe's SUV was made in relative silence. When they were safely ensconced in the vehicle, Moira gave a sigh of relief. "For a minute there, I thought we were going to be a special dog treat. We should say a prayer of thanks for that cat."

Joe's voice came out of the darkness. "Thank You, Lord, for nudging the cat out at that particular time. It was getting a bit hot in Jake's car."

Moira wondered how much of the prayer was serious and how much of it was simply Joe being funny. She was sure God didn't mind the humor, though.

"I have to say, Joe, things sure have livened up in the angel business since you've joined my efforts. Not that almost getting mauled by a dog is my idea of fun." Moira crossed her arms over her chest tightly and stared straight ahead. "I think I'm ready to go home now."

Chapter 4

Joe clamped his mouth shut. He should have known better. He'd had Moira on his mind when he returned home and had talked so much about her that now his mother wanted to get to know the new woman in her son's life. He knew the two women had met briefly at the yard sale when Moira purchased the desk, but they were merely acquaintances who attended the same church. He'd long admired Moira from afar and had often wished for an opportunity to get to know her better. God had provided it, and Joe was not going to waste it.

"Joe?"

He shifted his attention back to his mother.

"Yes?"

"I asked you when I could meet this woman."

"You've already met her," Joe pointed out. "At the yard sale. She bought your desk."

"I sold a hundred things to a hundred people that day. And much of what I sold was furniture. You can't expect me to remember every person I met."

"She attends Faith Church just like we do. You see her every week."

His mother tilted her head thoughtfully. "Moira Sullivan. . ."

"She helps with children's church," Joe mumbled.

"I don't have any children in children's church, Joe. Though I wouldn't mind having a grandchild or two there someday soon."

The grandchild ploy. He knew it well. Joe smiled. "I'd like that, too. In God's timing."

She nodded. "So how about dinner on Sunday? I could make that special—"

"I'll have to check with Moira, Mother. I'm not sure when she's available."

It wouldn't do to tell her he didn't think Moira would ever be ready for a visit with his mother. He loved his mother and knew Moira would, as well, once they got to know each other. Until that happened, however, he also knew his mother, who was very outgoing and interested in everything around her, could seem overwhelming.

Knowing what a private person Moira was, he suspected she would need to be introduced a bit gradually into his life and especially to his mother. They didn't yet have the kind of relationship that allowed for family eccentricities.

"Joe?"

He lifted his head again and found his mother staring at him.

"Hmm?"

"You haven't heard a word I've said. Where is your mind tonight? Are you going to invite your Moira for dinner Sunday?"

"She's not my Moira, but if the opportunity presents itself, I'll ask her."

"Where are we going tonight?" Joe glanced at Moira. She hadn't said a dozen words since he'd picked her up. He didn't think she was still annoyed that he'd asked her to join him and his mother for dinner on Sunday. She'd been almost too polite when she said she already had plans.

"I thought we'd stop by my friend Sarah's house tonight and deliver her angel. She's the chairperson of the social committee and is busy planning the

Christmas party. She's at a meeting right now, so we could put the angel in her mailbox."

"It's a federal offense to put unstamped mail into someone's home mailbox."

She stared at him. He felt the heat crawl up his neck and knew his face showed his discomfort.

"Only kidding. I mean, it really is a federal offense, but—never mind. That's fine."

Leave the lawyer shoes at home, Joe, he told himself.

"I wouldn't want to commit a crime," Moira said. "We can put it in her paper box. Is *that* illegal?"

Joe grimaced. He'd done it now. "That's fine."

They stopped directly in front of Sarah's mailbox since the newspaper box was attached to it. Moira wrapped the angel in tissue and set it toward the middle of the box, with the typed note telling Sarah it was a gift for her work in the Lord's service. This was a much smoother delivery than Jake Simon's had been. Joe smiled at the memory. Again, he wondered if that could be why Moira was so quiet. In hindsight, he thought the whole situation funny, but Moira didn't seem to share his opinion.

"Where to now?" he asked as Moira settled back into the passenger seat of his SUV.

"How about Gabe? Do you have any idea where

we could leave his angel?"

"Yes, I do." Joe grinned, turning the vehicle toward the road leading to the edge of town. "Gabe is a creature of habit. He comes to the church every Tuesday to clean the cross unless it's raining. Since the weather is nice today, he should be coming in about an hour. That leaves us plenty of time to put the angel up there."

"You want to put the angel on the roof?" Moira's eyes widened.

"Sure. Gabe keeps a ladder behind the bushes right where the cross is so he doesn't have to drag it out each week. He used a wooden one until recently. Now he has an aluminum one."

"I don't remember the last time I saw a wooden ladder."

"I think he made the wooden one himself. He was quite a carpenter in his youth. Identifies with Jesus the carpenter."

"Is that Gabe's occupation?"

"Not anymore. Gabe's retired. He used to make custom cabinets. Mom hired him years ago to redo the kitchen. He does meticulous work. Same way he cleans the cross. He's involved in other community projects, too."

"Gabe sounds like a nice man. I'm sorry I never

took the time to get to know him better."

"He's not dead. There's still time."

Moira smiled, which drew Joe's attention to her mouth. The shade of her lipstick very nearly matched the color of her perfect lips. He wondered what it would be like to kiss Moira. The way things were going, he feared he would never get that close to her.

"You're right. I'll make it a point to talk to him on Sunday."

Joe nodded, pleased to have been able to make a difference in a life, maybe two. Senior citizens needed friends just as much as anyone else did. Lifelong friends died. Spouses died. Those left behind had to go on, and he knew from watching his mother that it wasn't easy. His ears perked up as Moira spoke again.

"I don't know if I can climb up on the roof. I'm not good with heights."

"That's okay. I can do it. It was my idea."

"How will you get the angel to stay up there until Gabe arrives?"

Joe frowned. "Well, I don't know."

"Joe!"

He cringed at the exasperation in her voice. "I'm new at this subterfuge stuff. Let's just see how it goes. Something will come to me."

"You want to wait and see how it goes? What if it goes badly? Like some of the other times?"

"All of the angels were delivered, even if there might have been a snag or two. We haven't been caught." He suppressed the word *yet* that longed to attach itself to the end of the sentence.

Moira nodded slowly. "That's true. I know sometimes I'm too much of a perfectionist. God's working on me in that area. I'll try to be more flexible, but you'll have to be patient. And maybe you could think things through a bit, too."

"Okay."

He glanced at Moira as he drove along the familiar road. She twirled her fingers through the strands of her hair. It was strangely fascinating to him. He would have loved to sit there and simply watch her fingers twirl, but he had to keep his eyes on the road. He suddenly realized Moira was speaking again.

"I'm glad you brought up folks like Gabe. They don't get recognized for their work, and they should. When I began this project, I made only enough angels to cover the Sunday school teachers, deacons, and church staff. I think I might have already told you that."

"Yes, you did. You must have started working on

the angels as soon as you found Mother's—or had you already been making them then?"

"Your mother's angel gave me the idea, but I needed something that could be made faster and still look nice. So I had to design my own. Anyway, back to Gabe. It doesn't seem as though this has been planned out well. Maybe we should think about it some more."

Joe snorted. "Too much planning isn't good. Didn't you just say you were going to try to be more flexible? People have a tendency to do things unexpectedly. You have to adapt. There's always a way. Haven't you ever watched *MacGyver*?"

Her blank look told him she had no idea what he was talking about.

"MacGyver. The guy on TV who could disarm a missile with a paper clip or stop an acid leak with a bar of chocolate." He shook his head when Moira continued to stare blankly at him. "Never mind."

He sighed. The real reason he wanted to help Moira was because he wanted to spend more time with her, and this was a great way to accomplish that while doing something worthwhile. Unfortunately, he'd already flubbed the compatibility test—by questioning her methods, and in a hundred other ways, too.

He admired what Moira was trying to do. It wasn't

the first time he'd noticed her jumping in to help others. When the preschool moved to the newly constructed education building, Moira was right there, carrying boxes, setting up classrooms, even running to the local store for supplies that had been forgotten. He liked the way she gave of herself with joy. It was obvious to those around her that she didn't think of helping as an imposition but rather as a privilege.

Though she was quiet and reserved, she was a dedicated Christian. Her faith shone through in the things she did and the things she said. She was always encouraging, always ready with a smile. Always thinking of others over herself. In fact, Joe was impressed that she didn't seem to realize how much she contributed.

Following her example, he appreciated the chance to take his service to a higher level, to do more for both God and the church, but also for Moira. Being with her brightened his days and his life. She made him want to be a better man, to serve God and others just like she did.

As his thoughts tumbled in all directions, he realized why he was still single at thirty-four. He had never met a woman like Moira—a woman who wanted to serve God wherever He led, just as Joe himself served

Him. He had always believed God would one day show him the woman who would be his life's mate. With sudden clarity, he knew Moira could be that woman. Now all he had to do was convince her that he was the man for her.

"What made you decide to do this?" he asked.

She was silent for so long that Joe was afraid she wasn't going to answer, but after a few seconds, she spoke.

"I just felt led to contribute in some way." She paused, then continued. "It's a small thing, really. It takes about an hour or so to make an angel, which is why I spent that concentrated time making the extra ones. I still have my regular work to do to keep on target with my current deadlines."

Joe grinned. "You have deadlines?" He regretted the words almost as soon as he said them. To his own ears, his question sounded disrespectful of her job, and he hadn't meant it that way. He cleared his throat. "I mean, I didn't realize there were deadlines attached to designing."

Moira's voice was clipped as she responded. "If I want to eat, I have to produce. I have contracts for two books right now, and I have lessons to plan for the class I teach over at Barbara's Craft Shop. I'm scheduled to speak at a Crochet Guild convention in February. I have to get all the materials together."

As she warmed to her topic, her tone grew livelier. Her face flushed, and her slim hands moved in all directions as she talked. Did she realize how attractive all that energy and joy made her? A lump formed in his throat.

"You seem to enjoy your work."

"Yes, I do. Crochet has always been a part of my life. My mother taught me years ago, before she and Dad started having problems. It's helped me through a lot of tough times. I find it relaxing, and I love designing. Don't you love your work?"

"It's a paycheck." The words tumbled out without him thinking about them.

"A job should be more than a paycheck."

"Some are, I guess." He didn't really want to talk about work. Much of it he couldn't share because of confidentiality issues, but there was no way to stop her questions without being rude.

"If you don't enjoy it, why do you keep on doing it?"

Why did he? Joe spared a second to glance in her direction. He'd wondered the same thing himself on more than one occasion.

"I guess because it's what I was trained to do. I went to law school. I got a degree. I passed the bar. I practice law. It's what I do."

Moira opened her mouth but closed it before any words came out.

"What?" he asked irritably. He hated when people held back what they really thought. Clients did that often, usually when they were hiding something he wasn't going to like when he heard it.

"I was just going to say if you're not happy, you should find something that does make you happy. You're only what. . .thirty-five? You'll be working a long time. Why not do something that gives you pleasure besides income? Something you can be proud of."

"Thirty-four. Not everyone can have fun while they work. And I *am* proud of what I do." He could hear the irritation in his voice. This wasn't the way he wanted things to go. He wanted to get closer to Moira to enjoy the time with her, not cause dissension.

He had to admit that fun was part of the reason he'd wanted to do this. *And we will have fun.* He'd see to it. Moira would not regret letting him in on her project. A change of subject was in order. "So does your mother still crochet?"

He knew immediately it was the wrong thing to say. Moira's face fell.

"Yes, when she can. She can't afford a lot of extras since the divorce, and she won't accept my help."

"Have they been divorced a long time?"

"Since I was a teenager. They're not Christians, and when they began to have trouble, they didn't have the Lord to lean on. Things went from bad to worse."

"Marriage is certainly hard enough. Without God, I don't know how people do it." He paused, hoping a subject change wouldn't seem too abrupt. He didn't think Moira wanted to talk about her parents' situation. "Do you think we have enough angels now, or will you need to make more?"

She brightened some and nodded. "I think we do, but if I have to make a few more, it won't be a problem. I'm really glad you thought of adding these folks to the list."

It was the closest she'd come to saying she was happy he had joined the project.

"Glad to help." While he didn't need acknowledgment, he was pleased she wasn't regretting her decision to include him.

"Looks as though we've arrived."

Joe looked out the window and realized they had indeed arrived at the location of their next undercover angel adventure. He hoped this one went smoothly. Visions of Attila the Doberman flitted through his memory, and he sent up a whispered prayer that there would be no Attilas in this delivery.

Chapter 5

Moira felt somewhat better when they found the ladder just where Joe had said it would be—behind the bushes in front of the church, just under where the cross was attached to the wall. The cross was thick enough to hold the angel, so they wouldn't need anything with which to attach it, particularly since it wouldn't be up there very long.

Joe set the ladder close to the outer wall of the church, just even with the horizontal bar of the cross. The ladder was tall and reached almost to the top of the cross on the front of the building.

The cross itself was made of fiberglass and attached to the brick wall just below the point where the two sides of the roof met in the center. Because of an interest in the church history, Moira knew it was a Latin-style cross with three short arms and one long one, the style most associated with Christian churches. An outdoor floodlight brightened the white cross at night so anyone passing would be reminded of the Lord's sacrifice.

Standing in front of the cross, Moira realized it was larger than it had seemed at first. It was also higher.

"Are you sure you want to do this? We could think of another way to get Gabe his angel." Much as she wanted Gabe to have an angel, she didn't want Joe to get hurt. Of course, Gabe did this every week, but Gabe was used to it; and Joe was used to being in a courtroom, not on a ladder.

"Of course. It's not a problem. Look, I've made sure the ladder is secure, though you can stand here and hold it if it makes you feel better." He pointed to the ladder, waving his arm at it. "The rule is, you angle the ladder about a quarter of the total length. This ladder looks to be about sixteen feet, so I've angled it four feet from the wall."

"How do you know that?"

Joe laughed, the sides of his eyes crinkling with humor. "I have a roof, and I have a ladder. Just because I'm not a carpenter by trade doesn't mean I don't do any outdoor work. In fact, I enjoy working with my hands."

Moira felt the heat rush to her face. "I guess that didn't come out quite right."

"It's okay. We should get to it, though. Gabe could come by anytime now." Joe glanced toward the road and then up to the roof.

Moira nervously followed his gaze. "Maybe we should come back another time."

"Moira, we're here. We're doing it." He pulled a handkerchief out of his pocket. "I'll even clean off a spot so the angel won't get dirty."

"Good idea."

Resigned, Moira handed him the angel and positioned herself below the ladder, ready to steady it if needed.

Joe climbed up to what Moira thought was a ridiculous height.

"You don't have to go all the way up," she called.

Their eyes met as Joe looked down at her. "I know. But I thought it might not be so noticeable from below if it's at the top. It's white and would look like an extension of the cross."

It made sense, but Moira was still nervous, watching him balance on the ladder as he cleaned the spot where he was going to place the angel. She held tightly to the ladder, willing it to stay in place, her eyes on the rung in front of her.

"Moira!"

Joe's shout made Moira look up quickly. Was he falling? To her surprise, when she lifted her head, she saw Joe was no longer on the ladder. He had climbed to the roof.

"Gabe's early. Put the ladder down and come to the back of the church. Hurry."

Against her better judgment, Moira quickly returned the ladder to its hiding place where Gabe would hopefully not notice it had been moved. Though awkward to maneuver, at least the ladder wasn't heavy, which was probably why Gabe had opted to use this one.

She glanced toward the highway where Gabe was just pulling into the long driveway leading to the church parking lot. She quickly said a prayer that Gabe had not seen her removing the ladder or Joe on the roof. She hurried around the building, wondering how Joe was planning to get down from his perch.

When she arrived at the back of the church where Joe had parked his SUV, she found him sitting quietly on the lower edge of the roof.

He pointed toward his SUV and made driving

motions with his hands. Moira tilted her head as she attempted to figure out what he was trying to tell her.

Joe grimaced and pointed emphatically toward the SUV. Then he pretended to be driving and pointed straight down, where Moira was standing.

She could almost feel her eyes widen as she realized what he was asking. He wanted her to drive the vehicle underneath where he sat so he could use it to get down. How high was an SUV? Not as high as a ladder, she was sure. Joe was about six feet tall. Glancing at the SUV, she estimated it to be somewhere shy of six feet high. The single-story church building had eight-foot walls. There was a good chance if Joe could make it to the edge of the roof without falling, he would be able to make it to the roof of the car without injury. She hoped Gabe was so engrossed in his work cleaning the cross that he wouldn't pay attention to any noise they made. She wondered how long it would be before Gabe saw the angel.

There really wasn't a choice, however. Joe couldn't stay up on the roof forever. Moira determinedly made her way to the vehicle, slipped inside, and realized she didn't have Joe's keys. She walked back and looked up at Joe. He was dangling the keys from the end of his fingers, a smile on his lips. He motioned for her to back up, then threw the keys down in front of her. Moira cringed at the clanging noise that erupted in front of her as the multiple keys hit against one another. She could only be grateful they landed on the ground and not on the nearby cement.

Moira maneuvered the vehicle as close as she could get without hitting the bushes that surrounded the entire building. It was a good thing Joe had long legs, because he would need every inch of them for this.

Once she was in place, she turned off the engine and stepped outside, listening for sounds of someone coming to investigate the noise. Hearing nothing, she turned back to the wall of the building.

Moira held her breath as she watched Joe carefully descend to the edge of the roof, turn himself around, and very slowly ease himself over the edge to dangle close to the SUV. He stretched his legs to reach and dropped onto the luggage rack. A gasp escaped as she heard the soft plop of rubber shoes on metal.

Quickly moving toward him, she whispered, "Are you okay?"

Joe turned and slid off the car, then faced Moira. "I'm fine. And I didn't even dent the roof."

Moira rolled her eyes. "I was afraid Gabe would hear."

"Even if he did, he probably thought nothing of it. People are in and out of the church all day long." Joe slid into the driver's seat and started the vehicle. "Let's drive around to the front and go inside."

"What? Are you crazy?" After this close call, she couldn't believe he wanted to advertise their presence.

"As a loon," Joe said, chuckling softly.

"Joe!" She spoke as loudly as she could, with all the emphasis she could put into a loud whisper, but Joe paid her no heed. She slid into the passenger seat as Joe brought the SUV down the side street behind the church, out onto the highway, and back into the parking lot. He waved at Gabe, who was on the ladder, cleaning the lower portion of the cross. It didn't look as though he had found the angel yet, but it was hard to tell from this distance.

Joe slid out of the driver's seat and walked around to open the door for Moira. Again, she was impressed with his courtesy, much as she wanted to continue to be annoyed with him.

He leaned down and spoke softly in her ear. "If we're just arriving now, we couldn't possibly have put the angel on the cross, could we?"

Understanding dawned, and Moira nodded. The man was insufferably correct.

They walked inside, and Moira consulted Anne, the church secretary, about the preschool portion of the Christmas pageant, while Joe talked with the pastor about some legal matters. Moira had committed to helping the choir director, and since she was also part of the adult choir, she was doing double duty that night.

Joe had just returned to the office, when the outer door opened and Gabe came rushing in.

"Look. I got one. It has my name on it." Gabe's eyes were shining, and his face was flushed.

"One what, Gabe?" Anne asked.

"An angel. I got an angel."

He held it out, and Anne took it from him. Moira leaned in to have a look. It looked like the time outside had not harmed the angel any.

"It's just like the one I received a few weeks back—with your name on it and the little note and everything. Guess our undercover angel has been busy," Anne said. Anne then turned to Moira. "You should get one, too, Moira. You're always doing things for the church." Her eyes twinkled. "Better keep an eye out."

Moira laughed uneasily. Would she have to give herself an angel to keep suspicion away? The idea didn't sit well with her. "I don't do any more than anyone else." She turned to Joe and gave him a warning look. "Ready to go?"

Joe nodded, and they left together.

"That was exciting," Joe said as soon as they were out of earshot.

Moira sighed and turned slightly in her seat to face Joe. "Your idea of exciting is not the same as mine. I was scared to death you would fall off the roof. Why didn't you just climb down when you saw Gabe?"

"Not enough time. You needed time to move the ladder before he arrived."

"I admit that I would like to keep this anonymous, but not at the expense of your life."

"I wouldn't take that kind of chance. Trust me. Besides, even if I'd jumped off the roof, the most I'd have done was break a leg. It would hardly be life threatening. It's only one story high."

Moira sighed and looked out the window. Trust him. How could she do that? She didn't know Joe, not really. She knew he was a gentleman and a Christian. She knew he was successful at his job and he loved his mother enough to move in with her. Those were all good things. But she didn't really know him. She didn't understand how he could spend his days defending criminals and his weekends in church.

Joe's voice interrupted her thoughts. "Who's our next recipient?"

Moira stared out the window silently, contemplating the question. At the moment, she thought the best answer might be "no one."

Chapter 6

Each second of silence passed like an hour. Joe began to fear Moira was not going to answer his question. He hoped she wasn't having second or even third thoughts about his participation in this project.

"I can't do another one now. I have to go home and get ready for the Sunday school Christmas party."

Joe's heart did a flip as he realized God was giving him the perfect opportunity to take his relationship with Moira to a higher level. "I was planning to go, too. Why don't we go together?" He held his breath as he waited for her answer.

"I don't know. If people see us together. . ." Her voice trailed off, and Joe wondered what she was thinking.

"If you're worried about the angels, I don't see that as a problem. There's no reason for anyone to suspect the undercover angel is anything but a single person working alone. In fact, maybe going together would be a good cover. I think people should see us together. Isn't the party at Elizabeth Wright's house? The organist?"

"Yes. Elizabeth is a friend of mine. I was going to go early and help her set up."

"I'd be glad to add my hands if I can be of help."

"Well. . ." Her voice trailed off. Unable to resist, Joe glanced over at Moira to see the emotions flying across her face. His mind raced. He knew he'd better do some fast-talking if he were to convince her they should appear at the party together.

"Come on. You've seen how handy I can be." Perhaps he was pushing things, but he was desperate.

"I guess it would be okay."

Joe reined in the whoop he wanted to let out. He held his breath for a second before allowing himself to respond. "That's great. What time shall I pick you up?"

"Five would be good. Everyone is supposed to bring their favorite finger food. All I have to do is make punch and set up the plates and such."

"Isn't Elizabeth on the angel recipient list?"

Moira turned her head to look at him. "Yes," she said slowly. "What are you thinking?"

"We'll be right there in her house. With a lot of other people. Easy enough to drop an angel in her lap, so to speak."

Moira groaned, and Joe chuckled. At least she hadn't changed her mind. But for now, the mission of distributing the angels was of lesser importance. He had a date with Moira Sullivan!

From what Joe could see, the party was a tremendous success. The Wrights had a large, two-story home with an open area downstairs ideal for entertaining. They had obviously spent a lot of time decorating and getting the house ready for the party. It looked to Joe as though most of the church family was in attendance. He and Moira had decided that when Moira was ready to drop the angel in an inconspicuous spot, she would let him know and he would provide a distraction. In the meantime, he intended to spend as much time at her side as he could. He didn't know if it was good or bad that Moira didn't consider their being together a date, because he certainly considered it one.

He stood off to the side and watched her interact with the other guests. She could have been the hostess the way she made sure no one was left out. He could appreciate the effort she was making. Moira certainly had a mission heart.

Eventually she broke away from the group and headed his way. Joe straightened and waited, not wanting to seem anxious to have her at his side.

"What are you doing, standing here by yourself? Have you eaten?" she asked.

Her smile brought a smile to his own face. "Not yet. It looks like they have a nice spread, though."

Moira nodded. "Yes, they do. I'm starved, and I'm afraid I've done too much talking. My mouth is dry. Let's go get something."

His heart speeded up as Moira took his arm. Her touch, though light and friendly, caused his heart to speed up. Was it possible Moira could come to care for him? He was beginning to fear that when all the angels were delivered, he wouldn't see her again. It scared him how much he looked forward to being with her. He'd never felt this way about any other woman, but he wasn't sure if he was ready to make a long-term commitment. He had his mother to think about, too. The woman he chose for his wife must agree to having his mother in her home. Two women living under the same roof. He vaguely remembered a saying about that being trouble.

"Joe?"

He turned his head and smiled at Moira. "Yes?"

"I asked if you would like some of these chicken nuggets."

He glanced down at the food. "Sure. Why don't we each get a plate and just go around the table. Looks like there's enough to feed an army here. I was expecting chips and dip. I didn't realize they'd have actual food."

"Elizabeth loves to entertain. This is her one big bash of the year. Later she'll play the organ and we'll sing praise songs. She doesn't let anyone forget *why* we're celebrating."

"Sounds nice." Joe picked up a plate and began to add a few items to it.

A short time later, plates filled, they meandered back to the living room.

"Well, if it isn't Joe Corrigan."

Joe turned to see Clark Anvil, a prosecuting attorney with whom he often battled wits, coming toward him. He bit back a groan. He didn't want to talk shop tonight. He didn't want Moira to be bored. Yet he couldn't refuse to talk to the man.

"Clark. Nice to see you." What was he doing here anyway? Joe knew Clark didn't attend Faith Church.

Perhaps he was a friend of the Wrights. Assuming it wouldn't be polite to ask Clark what he was doing there, Joe simply extended his hand to the other man.

Joe glanced at Moira and found the smile she'd worn all night still in place.

"And who's this lovely lady making you look good?"

Joe maneuvered himself closer to Moira but turned so he could look at both her and Clark. "Moira Sullivan, this is Clark Anvil. He's also an attorney."

Moira nodded at Clark. "Merry Christmas, Mr. Anvil. How nice that you could be here with us this evening."

"Please call me Clark. Elizabeth was gracious enough to invite me. I didn't realize Joe would be here, though. You may not know this, but he's a formidable foe in the courtroom. We're usually on opposite sides. I can't say I'm ordinarily happy to see him. Have you ever seen him in action?"

Joe watched as Moira blinked and bit her lip. "Um, no, I haven't. I would imagine he's good at his job, though."

"Good? I'd say he is. If you ever have need of an attorney, I would recommend him."

"I hope I won't ever need one, not for the courtroom anyway." The smile remained on her face, but Joe sensed that Moira was uncomfortable with the topic.

Clark laughed loudly, and Joe cringed. "You've got a wise woman there, Joe," Clark replied.

A blush stained Moira's cheeks, and Joe wondered what part of Clark's statement embarrassed her. "She certainly is that," he said.

"Do you only work in the courtroom, Clark?" Moira asked.

"The courtroom is the final step. There's a lot of preparation that goes on beforehand, but of course we all have staff to help with that part. Right, Joe?"

"Actually, I prefer to do as much of the research myself as I can, though I obviously can't do it all. It helps me to understand my client better if I've done the background work. Then I know the case inside out." Joe squirmed. *Did that sound too pretentious?*

Clark snorted. "Listen to him. That's why you work so hard." He turned to Moira. "This guy could write his own ticket if he'd only take some of these high-profile cases." He shook his head. "I've never understood why you don't go after those, Joe."

"I can't properly defend a guilty client."

Clark splayed his hands out in front of him. "Everybody gets a defense, innocent or guilty. It's the law."

Joe nodded slowly. "Yes, it is. And I agree with it.

I just don't believe they would get the best defense from me if I knew my client was guilty." He kept his eyes focused on Moira, wondering what she thought of the turn of the conversation. "I realize there can be extenuating circumstances. . . ."

"You only defend the innocent?" Moira's voice was soft and hesitant. "How do you know they're innocent?"

Joe shrugged. "That's a tough call sometimes, but I do the best I can with a clear conscience."

Her smile disappeared, and a small frown creased her forehead. "But do you always have a choice?"

"I run a private practice. For the most part, I choose my clients."

"That's true," Clark said. "But if you want to build a career, there are political advantages to having your name well known, your reputation secure."

"I have no political aspirations," Joe said testily. It was true. He had never desired to go into politics. He was content with his lot as a defense attorney. In point of fact, he wanted to expand his services to help those who normally couldn't afford an attorney.

Clark shrugged. "To each his own. I'm just as glad to hear it. No competition when I jump in the ring." He turned to survey the room. "Time to shake some more hands." He faced Moira once again. "You two have a nice evening."

Moira's head bobbed up and down slowly. "You also."

When Clark was gone, conversation lagged. Joe wasn't sure what Moira's silence meant. Did she want to marry a man who was in the political arena? Did she think he was not ambitious enough? He didn't think she was the kind of woman who wanted the things a high-profile life would bring.

"It's pretty crowded," Moira said. "I think it's time to drop the angel. I saw a spot on the end table, just behind the picture of Elizabeth's twins, that will do."

"Okay. I'll provide your distraction. Give me a minute or two."

He walked off toward the grand piano in the corner of the room. He had an idea that might distract not only the guests but Moira, as well. He needed to salvage what was left of the evening.

Sitting down, he began to play one of the few songs he knew how to play, albeit badly. A few of the guests noticed and sauntered his way. He grinned. "Where's Elizabeth? It's been a long time since I've played. I don't think 'Chopsticks' is suitable for Christmas."

"There she is," someone in the crowd called out. With little coaxing, Elizabeth joined the crowd that now surrounded Joe.

"You do a much better job than I do," he told her with a smile, as he slid off the bench so she could sit down.

"But I've heard you sing, Joe. How about accompanying me? Do you have a favorite tune?"

Joe smiled. "Why don't we all sing?"

Moments later, Elizabeth began to play an introduction; and Joe positioned himself within eye contact of most of the guests and where he could also see Moira, who stood with her oversized purse open and ready.

At Elizabeth's nod, Joe opened his mouth and began to sing.

All heads turned his way. Some joined him, and others hummed along. Out of the corner of his eye, he saw Moira drop the angel onto the table and then step away to concentrate on the singing, along with the other guests.

Thank You, Lord, for this opportunity to worship You in such a setting. He closed his eyes as he poured out his heart to his Lord and Savior.

When the song ended, there was a hush as

everyone absorbed the meaning of the words they had sung. Then a burst of applause sounded.

Joe smiled and pointed to Elizabeth. "It's not me. It's the Lord who provided such fine accompaniment. Let's all gather round and praise Him for His mercy and love."

Elizabeth took the suggestion and began to play a song they had sung often in church services. Soon everyone was gathered around the piano, calling out songs. Elizabeth was an accomplished pianist and had no trouble keeping up. Joe felt more than saw Moira appear at his side. Seconds later, her hand was wrapped around his arm; and when he looked down at her, it was to find her looking up at him, a smile on her face as she sang out with the others.

Yes, this was the woman of his heart. The woman God surely wanted him to spend the rest of his life with.

Chapter 7

The Christmas spirit was in the air all around Moira as the church family gathered together for their annual celebration. A large Christmas tree stood in one corner of the room. This was the Angel Tree, which for weeks had been filled with cards, each one holding the name of a child in the local area. Moira was glad to see the tree was now bare, which meant that each of those children had been taken care of by someone in the church community.

Moira glanced first toward the front of the church, where the pastor was preparing to lead the service, then to the side where Joe's mother sat visiting with a neighbor. She spotted Joe kneeling down next to a little girl who was showing him a doll that Moira assumed she had received as a Christmas gift.

He glanced up, and their eyes met. Moira motioned casually to let him know she wanted to speak to him. Joe said a few words to the little girl and stood, turning to walk in Moira's direction.

"Hi. I'm glad you're here. I wanted you to meet my mother—officially."

Moira blinked. *Meet your mother? I don't think so.* Meeting his mother spoke of a closeness she wasn't quite ready for. She didn't say the words but rather pulled Joe to the side so they could talk privately.

"I brought an angel for the Nativity set."

It was Joe's turn to blink. "What Nativity set?"

"The one Manny and his family are going to put out as Pastor John reads the Christmas story." It was a tradition at Faith Church that the Nativity set was put up on Christmas Eve, each piece brought out as Pastor John read the story. Of course this year there would be no angel, since the original had been lost. Moira planned to fix that problem tonight.

"Oh. That's right. I heard the angel was missing in action. Ruined by a roof leak, wasn't it? Didn't they replace it?"

"It happened during the summer. Stores weren't selling angels then, and I think they meant to replace it later, but you know how that is. It was just forgotten.

Anyway, I heard Pastor John talking about it when I was at the church earlier. Someone had promised to get one but for some reason was unable to. The staff wasn't informed until the last minute. I had one angel left over, so—"

His eyes widened. "You're going to leave one of the angels tonight? With all these people here?" Then he laughed. "You surprise me, Moira."

Moira crinkled her nose at him. "We left an angel at Elizabeth's in the middle of a Christmas party. I think we can handle this."

A mischievous smile appeared on Joe's face. "You're right. What's the plan?"

"Follow me," Moira whispered.

She glanced around to make sure no one was paying attention, then moved casually to the front of the sanctuary, heading to the small room off to the left. Thankfully, it was empty. This room led to the choir room, which was open, but since the choir was not performing tonight, Moira assumed people would not be going in and out of the room.

"Here it is." She pointed to the Nativity set, which waited close to the doorway.

Joe studied the set thoughtfully. "Where do you want to put it?"

Moira stood in front of the Nativity set, examining it carefully. Her thoughts turned to the little babe asleep in the manger. What a life He had ahead of Him. The joy of childhood and then the pain of His undeserved death on the cross. She was grateful God loved her so much. The little she could do on this earth was nothing compared to what God had already done. She sighed.

"Here. Watching over the baby." It was the perfect place, of course.

She opened her purse and pulled out the angel with the shiny red heart sequin, the trademark of the undercover angel. *Angels,* she reminded herself. Joe was an undercover angel, too. She handed it to Joe, and he knelt to place the angel next to the manger where Manny would be sure to find it.

A soft gasp caused both of their heads to jerk up.

Two pairs of eyes widened as they saw Joe's mother standing in the doorway. Moira's heartbeat doubled. She looked at Joe, who stood quickly, his hand squeezing Moira's arm gently as he passed her to move to his mother, his hands motioning to quiet her.

"Mother, it isn't what you think—"

"It's you! You're the undercover angel. Or should I say 'angels'? My own son. And I never knew." Anna Corrigan shook her head. "I'm a crocheter myself, son. The angels are unique. I've been watching them pop up unexpectedly and admiring each one and how they're made." She frowned and then slapped his arm. "I can't believe you didn't tell me—"

"Moira wanted it to remain anonymous." His eyes narrowed as he looked at his mother. "And we *still* want it to remain anonymous."

Anna wouldn't meet his gaze.

"Mother." Moira could hear the warning in Joe's voice, but she knew there was nothing they could do to stop Anna from spreading the word if she decided to do so.

Anna walked past Joe and stopped at Moira's side. "I know you bought the desk at my yard sale, but I don't believe we've ever been formally introduced. I'm usually with the senior ladies, though I've seen you at church before, of course." She extended her hand. Moira gently laid her own hand inside it, and Anna gave it a hearty shake. "I'm Anna Corrigan. Nice to finally meet you, even if it was by accident." She turned slightly to include Joe in the conversation, her eyes boring into him. "Joe, have you invited Moira to the house after the service?"

"I was just going to do that," Joe began.

"No time like the present, son. You'll come, won't

you? The family is meeting there for supper. Well, everyone but Liza. She can't make it. My sister promised a big pot of hot chocolate to warm us up, though. Everyone is looking forward to meeting Joe's girl."

"Mrs. Corrigan—"

"Anna."

"Anna—" Moira hoped her feelings didn't show on her face. She didn't do well in crowds of people she didn't know, and she was still processing the shock of their being discovered in the act—by Joe's mother, no less.

"Moira may already have plans, Mother," Joe interrupted.

Moira turned to Joe. "It's not that. It's just. . ." Her voice drifted off as she tried to think of how to get out of the invitation without being rude.

"Will you be visiting with your parents, dear?" Anna asked.

Moira started, then frowned. "No. My mother lives in Denver, and my father lives in New Jersey. We haven't been together for Christmas in years." Even before the nasty divorce, they hadn't really been together. Her parents had married too young, before they knew what they wanted in life. Moira was determined not to make the same mistakes her parents had made. She would wait until she was ready to marry. She would wait for the right man, the man God chose for her. And she would know him a lot longer and a lot better than her parents had known one another.

"Then come and be a part of our family tonight. You can have a peaceful evening. No cooking, just eating and visiting." Looking at Anna's warm smile, Moira couldn't seem to make the word *no* come out of her mouth. The woman was sweet, even if pushy.

"All right. For a little while." It was a compromise, she told herself, a chance to convince Anna not to give away their secret. But if she was honest, she had to admit she wasn't quite ready to give up her last night in Joe's company. After all, she didn't have to marry the man to enjoy being with him for just one evening, did she?

Anna leaned to the side and spoke near Moira's ear. "That's a lovely dress, dear."

"Thank you." For some reason, the compliment unnerved Moira. Anna moved off, and Moira wondered yet again how she had ended up here, in Joe's living room on Christmas Eve.

She, Joe, and Anna had huddled together during the crowded Christmas Eve service. There had been some murmuring when the angel was put in place, but no one seemed to suspect her or Joe of being involved.

Surely Anna would keep their secret. Joe would see to it. He knew how important it was to Moira.

Joe. Though they had been partners in the under-cover angel venture, now that all the angels had been delivered, there was no further reason for them to get together. *Just in time,* she thought. Before things got out of hand and she became too dependent on seeing him. She had enjoyed spending time with Joe more than she thought she would. Though she was attracted to him in some ways, it was much too soon to think of a romantic relationship.

Moira wondered what her mother would think of Joe. Though her mother had married a lawyer, and their family had enjoyed the fruites of his labor, it had not turned out well for her parents. While having money was nice, Moira realized it was more impor-tant to have a man after God's own heart. A Christian who would put God at the center of his life and love his wife as Christ loved the church, just as the Bible says a man should. A man she could be sure of and could depend on in good times and bad. Not a man who would leave her after a few years as her father had left her mother.

She was sure God had a woman in mind for Joe, but she was just as sure she was not that woman. Though he was a good Christian and a good man, she didn't want to be involved with a lawyer, even if he did defend the innocent. And even if he claimed he had no political aspirations, he could change his mind and she could end up in the public eye.

Joe would find another woman to spend his life with. She frowned. Irritatingly, the thought of Joe with someone else made her want to squirm.

If Clark could be believed, Joe didn't go after his cases based on what they could do to further his career. She and Joe hadn't discussed it, but as she'd gotten to know Joe better, she realized he had a high work ethic. He believed in justice. And he trusted God. Moira felt her lips lift in a small smile. One would have to trust in the Lord, given how many times they'd almost gotten caught delivering angels.

A touch at her elbow brought Moira back to the present. Joe was standing beside her, a grin on his face. "Sorry. Pastor John had some questions about the church property sale. He's anxious to get started on the new building for the preschool, and this was the first step. We kept missing each other during working hours. This was my first opportunity to talk with him."

"I thought you were a criminal lawyer."

Joe's eyebrows rose. "I defend the accused. I wouldn't call them criminals." He shook his head. "Even so, I know a bit about other aspects of the law. This is a pretty straightforward sales contract, but I told him I'd have a buddy of mine look it over, just to be sure."

Moira nodded. She couldn't help admiring the way Joe looked. The blue background of his sweater brought out the blue in his eyes, while the snowflakes reminded her of past Christmases, before her parents divorced. Snow was a rarity in the South, but when she'd lived in Colorado, she could look out her window at mountains topped with white. The navy blue dress pants allowed Joe to keep his lawyer image despite the snowman on his chest. Of course she knew he was the same person no matter what kind of clothes he wore, but his more casual outfit made her forget for a little while what he did for a living. The more she knew of Joe, the more she saw the kind of person he was—one with a great deal of honor and love for others.

"It's nice of you to help him out even though it's Christmas Eve."

"I didn't mind."

They were quiet, both watching the group of people moving around the room. Anna roamed from group to group, making sure everyone had something to eat or drink, much like Moira did when she was with her own friends.

"Remember when. . ." Joe's soft voice rolled over her as he began to reminisce about the delivery of Jake's angel and their run-in with the Doberman.

"Did you ever find out what happened to the dog?" Moira asked.

Joe nodded, leaning in closer so they wouldn't be overheard. "Animal control picked him up soon after we called it in. Turns out the dog was let out accidentally. The owners picked him up at the pound that same night."

"Good. I'm glad he didn't have us for supper, though."

"I have to agree with you there."

A soft chuckle escaped from Joe's throat, and Moira smiled. She liked being able to make him laugh. She'd never been good at telling jokes, nor did she have anyone to share them with, even if she were a comedienne. Joe had changed her—for the better.

Joe sighed, and a shadow crossed his face. Moira tilted her head as she watched him.

"Is something wrong?" she asked.

"Wrong?"

She shrugged. "Never mind. You just had this look on your face."

He suddenly seemed uncomfortable and shuffled from one foot to the other. He must have realized what he was doing, as he suddenly stopped and resumed their conversation. "I was just thinking about our adventures delivering the angels. Did we accomplish all you'd hoped?"

She lowered her voice, remembering that some of these people were members of their church. "All the angels were delivered. I think we did well, partner."

"It certainly gave the church something to talk about for a few months. It's almost a shame to see it come to an end."

Yes, a shame, she thought, but she didn't say it. Out loud, she said, "I think we covered everyone we could in the time we had."

"I think so, too. There's always next year, or maybe we could do something for Easter."

Moira felt the blood drain from her face. This was just what she'd been afraid of. Joe wanted to extend their partnership. "Next year?"

"Sure. There's no reason to give it up, since you obviously enjoy it so much. It could become a Christmas tradition at Faith Church."

"I don't think that's a good idea."

"Why not? Didn't you have fun?"

"Sometimes it was fun. Sure."

"I know we sort of started off on the wrong—"

"Moira. Come and say hello to everyone." Anna suddenly appeared beside them. She put her arm around Moira and pulled her into the center of the room where a group of women stood waiting. "This is Moira Sullivan. She's here with Joe. She crochets for a magazine." Anna turned and motioned toward another woman who appeared to be about Moira's age. "This is Joyce, Joe's cousin. She crochets, too."

With Anna leading the conversation, Moira soon found herself involved in a discussion of designing and the process of publishing. Moira noticed Joe easing his way to a gathering of young men, where he became involved in a conversation of his own. She didn't see much of him the rest of the night, though their eyes often met. He would give her a smile, and she wondered if he knew her discomfort at being the source of attention in a group of people she didn't really know. Yet she was surprised at how easily she adapted to Joe's family. While she expected her own friends to ask about her work, these people didn't know her, yet they seemed genuinely interested in what she had to say. Still, she knew Joe's relatives considered them a couple, and that wasn't true. She felt a twinge of guilt at not setting them straight.

After a while, Joe appeared at her side. "Ready to escape?" he whispered.

She nodded, continuing to smile at the young girl with whom she was talking.

"Sorry, Judy, time for us to head out," Joe said.

Everyone expressed regret as they made their way to the door, but Moira was aware of winks and smiles among the company.

Regardless of what his family wanted, Moira knew she had to make sure Joe understood that theirs had been a partnership of convenience and she was not ready for or interested in anything more. She cared for him as a brother in Christ, and she thought they'd become friends; but nothing more serious could come of it—at least not now.

They drove in silence to her home, but the silence was not an uncomfortable one. Rather, Joe put the car heater on to ward off the stiff December chill, and Moira was content just to sit and enjoy the quiet. She knew she should bring up their earlier conversation, but she couldn't seem to make herself shatter the peace.

Joe pulled up at the curb and walked around the

car, as she'd come to expect. She sat waiting until he opened the door for her.

"Thank you," she murmured.

She took his hand and slid out of the passenger seat. He didn't relinquish her hand but held on to it as he walked her to her door.

"I hope my relatives didn't annoy you too much."

Moira looked up at him. The streetlight cast a glow so she could see Joe's face, though part of it was in shadow. She knew she had to say something. Yet still she hesitated. The sound of Snowflake barking at the door gave her a few seconds to think.

"He's happy you're home," Joe said, tilting his head in the direction of the door with a smile.

"Yes. But when I go inside, he'll curl up and go right to sleep." She knew she still hadn't answered his question. He was giving her an out by changing the subject; but she'd really had a good time, and she wanted him to know it. "I enjoyed meeting everyone at the party. They're an interesting group, and they were all nice. I didn't feel too out of place."

"I'm glad, because I was serious earlier about continuing our partnership. But I don't really want to wait until next Christmas to deliver angels, though we certainly can do that."

"Joe," Moira began, "I've enjoyed delivering angels with you, but I thought I'd made it clear from the beginning that that was all it was. You gave me little choice, as you recall. We were partners. But the angels are delivered now, and while I'd certainly like to remain friends, I don't think I'm ready for anything more than that."

"I see." She thought he did see, because his face fell. Her heart beat faster. He still held her hand, and now he lifted it to his lips and kissed it. "I'll respect your wishes, but, Moira, I'll ask you to pray about it. While I don't presume to speak for God, you've been on my heart, and I think God isn't through with us."

Moira forced a smile to her lips. "I know He's not finished with me. I have a long way to go."

"We all do. You know that's not what I meant."

He pursed his lips and looked at her, his eyes sad and his shoulders drooping.

Moira suddenly felt an inch tall. "I'm sorry. I don't mean to make light of it."

"Is it me particularly you don't want to have a relationship with? Is there something about me that puts you off?"

Moira hesitated as she remembered the first time Joe had visited her home. She gently pulled her hand away from his. "I admit I was concerned about your occupation."

"You don't date lawyers?"

She turned to her right so she didn't have to look him in the face. "I haven't dated any lawyers except you." Moira took a deep breath and lifted her eyes to his. "You remember I told you I'd been in a courtroom before? What I didn't tell you is that my father is a lawyer. Whatever else he's done, he shines in the courtroom." She sighed. I don't understand how a Christian could defend a person who has committed a crime. I know you tried to explain, but I'm not sure I really understand even now."

Joe shuffled his feet and sighed. "As I told you before, as far as I can tell, the people I defend *are* innocent. It's not always easy to tell, and sometimes I make a mistake in judgment. When that happens, I'm honor bound to give the best defense I can regardless. That's the way our system is set up. Innocent or guilty, everyone gets their day in court. I don't defend my occupation. It's what I do. I'm sorry if that's a problem."

His speech left her feeling guilty somehow. "I'm glad you've chosen to help the innocent, but I can't help the way I feel. My father's occupation and his political aspirations were a part of their later problems. I know you've said you're not interested in politics, but you may change your mind one day."

"I doubt that, but God controls the future. Not me. If He led me that way, I guess I'd go." Joe sighed deeply. "This is it then. It's been nice working with you," he said stiffly.

He stepped back and waited while she opened her door.

She picked up Snowflake and watched from her doorway as Joe walked slowly back to his car and drove off.

Her heart sank as she realized what she'd done. She'd sent him away. Joe Corrigan was finished with Moira Sullivan, by her own choice. It was what she wanted, wasn't it?

Merry Christmas. Her eyes welled with tears. What was wrong with her? It was the right decision. She remembered quite well what had happened to her parents. She knew it happened over and over again to many others, as well. People threw relationships away as they did old clothes. She didn't want that. She wanted a relationship that was God-centered and life-long. It took time to build that kind of relationship. If her parents had taken that time, perhaps they could have weathered their problems.

There was time for that to happen. She was still a young woman, and there was no hurry to marry. Maybe Joe felt the same. Maybe when she was ready, Joe would be ready, too. *Maybe.*

She closed the door, set Snowflake back on the floor, and walked to the bedroom. Slowly she lay down on the feather bed she had impulsively treated herself to just last month. Closing her eyes, she allowed herself to enjoy the softness beneath her, remembering all the good things the television salesperson had said about the bed. Then she turned over and reached to her nightstand for her Bible. There was only One who would be able to help clear her thoughts. The One who cared for her more than anyone else could. He would never lead her astray. She could trust Him with her life and her love.

She fell asleep, the Bible still in her hands.

Chapter 8

M oira walked into the church, accepted a bulletin from the greeter at the front door, and proceeded to the fellowship hall. The first Sunday in February was her class's turn to provide breakfast. The informal meal was also a time to welcome new church members and for present members to catch up with one another. As was her custom, Moira filled a cup with coffee, sugar, and a bit of milk, grabbed a doughnut, and turned to see which of her classmates had arrived. Sarah was in a group at the other side of the room, so Moira headed in her direction. As she got closer, Sarah looked up, her eyes widened, and a pink tinge ran up her neck. Moira paused, confused, but then Sarah motioned for her to join them.

"Moira." Sarah greeted her a little too enthusiastically. The other class members turned, mumbled a greeting, and moved off to get seats.

"Was it something I said?" Moira tilted her head and looked at her friend.

"Of course not." Sarah's voice was unconvincing. "It's just that it's almost time to start. Let's get a seat." Sarah led the way, and Moira sat down beside her.

Throughout the class, however, Moira had the feeling people were looking at her. When she glanced around the room, faces quickly turned away. It was an unsettling feeling. She was obviously an object of interest today. She was glad when the bell rang and class dispersed. She realized she hadn't gotten much out of today's lesson.

She was moving quickly toward the door when, suddenly, Sarah grabbed Moira's arm and pointed. "Oh, look, there's Joe Corrigan."

Moira gazed in the direction Sarah motioned. There was Joe, standing in the aisle, holding a young child and talking to a woman, whom Moira assumed was the child's mother. Joe was laughing, and though he was too far away for her to see them, she could picture how his blue eyes crinkled when he chuckled. Joe enjoyed life and laughed often. He'd made her laugh, too, and she missed that.

Joe leaned over and kissed the cheek of the woman he was talking to, and then the two of them slid into a pew, continuing their conversation. The child laid his head on Joe's shoulder and appeared to be going to sleep.

"Let's go over and say hello," Sarah continued.

But Moira hung back. "No. It's almost time for the service to begin. Besides, I need to wash my hands. They're sticky from the doughnuts." Any excuse was better than having to meet Joe's new love interest.

Moira quickly moved off in the direction of the ladies' room, and Sarah followed. Moira frowned as she hit the soap dispenser.

"I didn't know you knew Joe Corrigan," she said casually as she turned on the faucet and stuck her hands beneath the spray of water.

Moira watched Sarah's face in the mirror and saw a light blush form over her face.

"I don't know him. I thought you did," Sarah said. She glanced at her watch. "It's time for the service to start. We'd better get going."

They hurried to the sanctuary, but Sarah paused at the entry, looking around the room. "There's Joe. Do you want to go sit with him?" she asked.

Moira stared at her. "Why would I want to do that?" *Particularly since he's with another woman.* She turned to face her friend. "Sarah?"

Sarah sighed. "You could have told me. I'm your best friend." She shrugged. "Oh, forget it. Let's just find a seat."

Sarah moved into a pew before Moira could gather her wits to respond to her friend's strange statement. Moira joined her on the seat and stared at the words in the bulletin, but her eyes wouldn't focus. Sarah seemed to think she and Joe were a couple. Why? She didn't recall seeing Sarah at the Christmas party at Elizabeth's house. That was the only time Joe had been with her in public. Maybe someone else had seen them together there and commented on it. Moira knew rumors sometimes developed a life of their own. Were the church members talking about them as a couple?

A couple. Of course they weren't a couple. Joe was here with another woman. Moira's mind whirled. *Doesn't Sarah think that's strange?*

Moira sighed deeply. Thoughts of her time with Joe wouldn't leave her. She had about given up fighting it. No matter how hard she pushed the images from her mind, they immediately returned. She couldn't believe thoughts of him were still stuck in her head like this.

Moira rubbed her temples. A headache threatened to overwhelm her. She felt a lump in her throat. Joe had moved on. She'd told him in so many words that she wasn't ready for a relationship. Apparently Joe was ready for one, and in the short weeks since they'd last spoken, he'd taken steps to find a woman who shared his desires.

A whine sounded from the microphone as the pastor began to make the announcements, and Moira forced her attention to the front of the church. She stood with the rest of the congregation as they began to sing praise and worship songs. Though she tried, she found she couldn't join in the singing. The words caught in her throat, and her voice cracked. She moved her eyes over the words and took them into her heart. The song was about God working things out when there didn't seem to be any way things could work. Would God make a way for her? And if He did, where would that way lead? Was it too late for her and Joe?

Moira knew that God was always at her side. She constantly relied on His strength and love. But she also felt that God expected each one to do his or her part. She had turned Joe away. What if God had put Joe in her path for a different reason than delivering angels? What if God meant Joe to be her future husband and she had turned her back on His will? How could she be sure? And did it even matter? Joe was with another woman. She had no right to change her mind now.

Trying to focus on the sermon, Moira found that her thoughts kept drifting as her eyes caught sight of Joe. His attention was on the pastor, and he appeared to be drinking up the words of the sermon. Moira sighed.

She realized how much she missed Joe. It wasn't just the fun they'd had delivering angels she missed. It was the encouragement, the support, the caring. She pictured Joe walking around the car to open the door for her. Such a small thing, and yet it was just another extension of his personality.

Even if she wanted to begin a relationship with Joe, it was too late. She'd pushed him away, causing a distance between them. Joe was respecting her wishes. He had not contacted her since Christmas, though he'd been polite and friendly whenever they ran into each other at church. He had other things in his life besides her. His actions did not depend on her, nor did she affect his decisions.

Right now, however, she needed to put her mind where it should be. She was in the house of the Lord and needed to concentrate on Him. *Help me to focus, Lord. You deserve my entire concentration.* Determined, she opened her Bible and focused on the pastor.

"Hey, Joe."

Joe glanced up and moved to the side to make room for Manny Wiseman and his wife.

"Who you got there?" Manny whispered.

"This is my nephew, Aaron." Joe patted Aaron's back. His sister, Liza, had come for an unexpected visit, and Joe was happy beyond measure that she'd agreed to attend church services with him. Since her husband died, she'd pulled away from the Lord. This was the first time she'd been open to renewing that relationship, and Joe determined he would do everything he could to make her comfortable here and encourage her to open herself to God's healing powers.

"Getting a little practice in before having one of your own, huh?"

Joe looked at Manny, for once at a loss for words. *What a question.* He wasn't even dating anyone, and Manny was asking if he was preparing for a family of his own. Manny looked away from Joe, and Joe followed his gaze to see Moira sitting across the aisle.

As he held little Aaron, Joe admitted to himself

that he did yearn for a family of his own. He'd hoped Moira would be the mother of his children. He thought he was doing God's will when he approached her about a relationship. How could he have been so wrong? Could it be true that Moira really didn't have any feelings for him?

He again looked across the aisle at the woman of his dreams. Her eyes were focused on the front of the church. Did she ever think about the time they'd spent together?

He sighed deeply, knowing he should be paying more attention to the pastor and less to his own thoughts. God would take care of everything. Whatever happened, if God was in it, it would be right. He had to trust the Lord.

One thing he did know was that he wouldn't push Moira. If she wasn't ready, if she didn't want a relationship, whether with him or anyone, he wouldn't force the issue. He knew, however, that it would be a long time before he felt the same way about another woman.

The service was about to conclude, and for the first time in his life, Joe was anxious to leave the church building. Being so close to Moira and unable to talk to her, except for a simple greeting, was driving him crazy. He wasn't sure if he would be able to maintain his distance if he stayed at Faith Church. Perhaps it was time for a change.

Pastor John walked to the front of the church, replacing the song leader at the podium.

"Today there is something special I'd like to say."

Joe's ears perked up at the unusual opening. Though he was quite active in the church and a personal friend of the pastor, he had no clue what was coming.

"You all know that myself and members of the church staff received special gifts during the past Christmas season." He paused. "These gifts were delivered anonymously, with a note of encouragement addressed to each recipient." He looked around the room, and Joe felt the heat of a blush crawl up his neck as the pastor seemed to look directly at him. "Philippians 2:3 says, 'Do nothing out of selfish ambition or vain conceit, but in humility consider others better than yourselves.' I think those who provided this message of hope and encouragement took this verse to heart."

Pastor John moved to front center stage as he talked. "Though the angels were delivered anonymously, someone has already let the cat out of the bag. I think most of you know who these good-hearted people are, so I don't think I'm stepping on any toes by talking about it. I think it is important their generosity is publicly recognized in this time when it seems honesty and integrity are in short demand, when instant gratification is the mode of the day, and most focus on their own needs. They have shown us there are still those who think of others above themselves." He smiled, and his eyes moved from one side of the church to the other. "An angel gave the good news about Jesus' birth to the shepherds, guiding them to Joseph and Mary in Bethlehem. Our undercover angels brought the good news of hope and encouragement to everyone here in this church by their selfless acts." He smiled. "Moira Sullivan and Joe Corrigan, I just want to say thank you, on behalf of all the recipients of the beautiful angels you provided us."

As the church family broke into applause, each one turning to locate Joe and Moira among the congregation, Pastor John moved back and the song leader nodded to the organist to begin the final hymn.

Joe was grateful Pastor John hadn't called them to stand with him, though he wasn't sure if it was any better to have their names announced to the congregation. He tried to see how Moira was taking the news, but she remained facing the front. She would be furious, he knew, and she would know how the pastor discovered their secret. There was only one person, other than the two of them, who knew the truth about the undercover angels. His mother.

Chapter 9

Moira forced a smile to her face as she tried to leave the church. She'd never known it could be so hard to smile. People kept stopping her to ask about the angels. She repeated the story a dozen times, each time condensing it just a little bit more. She now had it down to about a half dozen sentences. Inside, she fumed. How could this happen? No one knew. No one. Well, Joe knew. She frowned. And Joe's mother.

That was it. It was Anna. It had to be. She'd told someone, or many someones, and the news had gotten to the pastor. She'd almost died when Pastor John thanked her and Joe for delivering the angels, essentially telling everyone that they were the under-cover angels. She couldn't be angry with him, though, because she now understood why Sarah and the other women in her Sunday school class were talking about her. It wasn't about her romantic relationship with Joe but about her and Joe delivering the angels together.

Her head ached. Maybe they were talking about both. It would be logical for people to assume they were working together because they were a couple, even if that wasn't the way it was.

She couldn't let people continue to think that. Joe would be upset, and so would his girlfriend, yet she didn't know how to set things straight. She would have to talk to Joe about it.

"Moira."

She whirled around at the familiar voice. Joe stood not two feet in front of her. Another step and she would have walked right into him.

"Joe."

"I'm sorry. I know you didn't want this to get out. I'll talk to Mother. It had to be her. No one else knew." He spoke softly. She assumed he didn't want to say anything negative about his mother in the crowd of church members, many of whom knew the family.

"Never mind. It's out now. It can't be undone. Just let it go." It wasn't exactly what she felt, but she knew it was the right thing to say; and she knew she *would* feel that way eventually.

Joe took her arm and gently led her out to the parking lot. The crowd moved off as soon as Joe took her away, as though they understood the two of them needed time alone. Time alone for what, she didn't know, as there wasn't much else that could be said.

"I know you're angry," Joe began.

"Shocked. Surprised. Yes, angry. But I will get over it."

"I can only apologize. I had no idea Mother told anyone. She's home with a cold today, but I will talk to her. As you've already said, however, it can't be undone."

She realized Joe didn't fully understand why she was really upset. She had to set him straight. "Joe, people think we're a couple."

His eyes narrowed. "I don't see why, but if they do, we'll set them straight on that. But. . .would it be such a bad thing?" His smile almost undid her.

"Of course it would! Won't your girlfriend be angry?" Moira frowned, nonplussed at his attitude.

"What? My girlfriend?" His eyebrows rose. "What girlfriend?"

Moira took a deep breath and motioned toward the woman in question, who was walking across the parking lot toward Joe's car, carrying the little boy Joe had been holding.

Joe turned his head to look where she was pointing. Then he burst out laughing.

Moira's shoulders slumped. This wasn't funny. Joe had a terrible habit of laughing at things that weren't funny to her. Didn't he realize how this would look to another woman? Maybe he didn't. Men were a bit dense sometimes about things like this.

"She isn't my girlfriend," Joe finally managed.

"She's not?"

"No, Liza's my sister. Come on. I'll introduce you." He started off toward the woman and child, but Moira stayed where she was. When he realized she wasn't following him, he turned back. "What's wrong?"

"I—thank you, but no. Please give her my apologies, but I need to go." Moira suddenly felt as though all the air in the parking lot had been sucked into the clouds above. Her heart and head were both pounding. She had to get out of there.

Joe was not seeing another woman. Joe was still free. And she was back in the fire—with a decision to make.

She swung her car door open and slipped behind the steering wheel, started the car, and headed out of the parking lot without a backward glance.

Joe stomped from one end of the living room to the other. Liza gave him a threatening look, and he set his feet down more gently as he paced the room. Aaron was sleeping, and it wouldn't do to have a grouchy two-year-old in the house.

He couldn't get Moira out of his mind. He'd talked to his mother, and she admitted telling one of her friends about the angel deliveries; but she seemed honestly surprised the news had traveled so far. She apologized profusely and offered to apologize to Moira, as well. Joe wasn't sure if that was a good idea or not. Moira hadn't taken the announcement well. He was sure she would never speak to him again, and the thought pained him more than he could say.

Even after she had told him she wasn't ready for a relationship, he still harbored the hope that one day she would be ready and that she would consider him in that light. He was sure they could work out her problems with his job. To be honest, he wasn't all that happy with it either. He'd been toying with other ideas lately, and maybe this was as good a time as any for a change. He would have liked to consult with Moira before he made any decisions, however, but now it didn't look like that was going to happen anytime soon.

The doorbell rang, and he growled. He didn't want to see anyone, but he couldn't let the person continue to ring the bell and wake up Aaron. Mother was resting, and a quick glance told him his sister was on the phone.

He hurried to the door, forcing down his annoyance so he could greet their guest properly. However, when he swung open the door, no one was there.

Frowning, he glanced up and down the sidewalk, thinking perhaps the person had thought no one was home and walked away. But no one was in sight. Then the sun reflected off something shiny on the top step leading to the doorway.

An angel.

Not just any angel, but an angel with a shiny red heart sequin.

He remembered the first time he'd visited Moira and his comment about an angel appearing on Gabe's doorstep. He squatted down and lifted the angel from its perch. He knew they had given out all of the angels Moira had made. She must have made this one especially for him.

What was she trying to tell him? The other angels

had been delivered to give hope and encouragement. He smiled as he stood, bringing the angel with him. Was that the message meant for him?

He lifted his eyes and noticed Moira's white car, parked nearby. Moira stood next to the car, waiting.

She wouldn't have to wait long. Long strides took him to her side in seconds.

"Hey." He placed his finger under her chin and lifted her face so he could see her eyes. He didn't know what else to say. He hoped she would talk. . .explain. His heart hammered against his ribs.

Her eyes were sparkling. "I wanted to deliver angels to show how much I appreciated the church workers. Well, there's one church worker who didn't get one. Someone I appreciate more than any of the others. Someone who was always there for me, who taught me how to laugh, who loves the Lord above all else. Someone who captured my heart, despite my best intentions." She smiled as she said the last, and Joe returned her smile.

"But he's a lawyer," he pointed out, his tone tentative.

She laughed and winked. "Well, not just any lawyer."

"I love you," he said softly. Lowering his face, he touched her lips with his, gently savoring the kiss.

"I love you, too, Joe Corrigan."

He pulled her to his side. "Let's go. I think we have a lot to talk about."

Walking beside the woman who had stolen his heart, Joe thought he was the luckiest man alive. *Thank You, Lord.*

Moira's Angel

For more detailed instructions, please visit my Web site at www.sandrapetit.com.

Materials: Small amount worsted-weight white cotton yarn; F crochet hook; #16 needle; white chenille pipe cleaner; small red heart sequin

Size: 5½ inches tall with 5-inch wingspan

Skill level: Intermediate

Time: 1½ hours

Special stitches: Shell = 3 dc; corner = (shell, ch 3, shell)

ABBREVIATIONS

beg = beginning	sc(s) = single crochet(s)
ch = chain	shell = 3dc
dc(s) = double crochet(s)	sl st = slip stitch
dec = decrease	sp = space
hdc = half-double crochet	st(s) = stitch(es)
hk = hook	wk = work
rnd = round	yo = yarn over

BODY

Make a 3-round granny square as follows:

Ch 5, join with sl st to form a ring.

Rnd 1: Ch 3, work 2 dc in ring, (ch 3, shell in ring) three times, dc in top st of beg ch 3.

Rnd 2: (Ch 3, 2 dc, ch 3, shell) in same sp, (ch 1, in next ch 3 sp wk corner) three times, hdc in top of beg ch 3 (8 shells).

Rnd 3: (Ch 3, 2 dc) in same space, (corner in next ch-3 sp, ch 1, shell in next ch-1 sp) three times, then ch 1, corner in next ch-3 sp, ch 1, join with sl st to top of ch 3, finish off, leaving a long end loose for sewing sides together (12 shells).

 With right side facing you, corner at the top, fold sides so they meet in the center to form a cone shape. There will be a "skirt" hanging lower than the rest. Starting at top, leaving the top ch 3 open, insert needle in first dc of first shell and whipstitch sides together. Finish off. Sew in ends. Turn piece inside out, pulling right side to the front.

Border: Holding body upside down, attach yarn with a sl st in sp to left of center joining at bottom of skirt. Ch 3, 2 dcs in same sp. Skip first dc of next shell. In center dc of that shell, wk 1 sc, (shell in next sp between shells, skip one dc, 1 sc in next dc) twice. At point of skirt wk 5 dc, skip next dc, in next dc wk 1 sc, (shell in next sp, skip one dc, 1 sc in next dc) twice, shell in final sp, join to top of beginning ch. Finish off. Sew in ends on *wrong* side.

WINGS

Special Stitch: Sc dec: Insert hk in st, yo, pull through (2 loops on hk), insert hk in next st, yo, pull through, (3 loops on hk), yo, pull through all 3 loops.

Row 1: Ch 11, sc in 2nd ch from hk and in each ch across (10 scs).

Row 2: Ch 1, turn, sc in each st across (10 scs).

Row 3: Ch 1, turn, sc in first st, sc dec over next
2 sts, sc in next 4 sts, sc dec over next 2 sts,
sc in next st (8 scs).

Row 4: Repeat row 2 (8 scs).

Row 5: Ch 1, turn, sc in first st, sc dec over next
2 sts, sc in next 2 sts, sc dec over next 2 sts,
sc in next st (6 scs).

Row 6: Repeat row 2 (6 scs).

Row 7: Ch 1, turn, sc in first st, (sc dec over next
2 sts) twice, sc in next st (4 scs).

Row 8: Repeat row 2 (4 scs).

Row 9: Ch 1, turn, (sc dec over next 2 sts) (2
scs).

Row 10: Repeat row 2 (2 scs).

Row 11: Ch 1, turn, (2 sc in next st) twice (4
scs).

Row 12: Repeat row 2 (4 scs).

Row 13: Ch 1, turn, sc in first st, 2 scs in next
2 sts, sc in last st (6 scs).

Row 14: Repeat row 2 (6 scs).

Row 15: Ch 1, turn, sc in first st, 2 scs in next st, sc
in next 2 sts, 2 scs in next st, sc in last st (8 scs).

Row 16: Repeat row 2 (8 scs).

Row 17: Ch 1, turn, sc in first st, 2 scs in next st, sc

in next 4 sts, 2 scs in next st, sc in last st (10 scs).

Row 18–19: Repeat row 2 (10 scs), do not finish off.

Border: Ch 1, turn, 3 sc in first st for corner, sc in next 8 sc. Insert hk in last stitch (corner st), yo, pull through (2 loops on hk). Place chenille stem along side (this will be top of wing); with hk above stem, yo and pull through, completing a sc. Wk 2 more sc in same st. Sc in each row along side, covering stem as you go. Bend stem as needed to follow shape of wing. At end of row, wk 1 sc in corner st, clip leftover stem (at both ends) being careful not to clip threads, then complete 2 more sc for corner. Sc in next 8 sts, working over loose strand so you don't have to sew it in later, wk 3 scs in corner, 1 sc in each row along side. Join with a sl st. Finish off. Sew in ends.

HEAD

Rnd 1: Ch 4, join with sl st to make a ring, ch 3, wk 9 dcs in ring, join with sl st to top of beg ch (10 dc).

Rnd 2: Ch 1, wk 1 sc in same st, (2 scs in next st) around, join with sl st to top of beg ch. Finish off. Sew in ends.

HALO

Starting about half an inch in, wk scs around stem
of 6-inch piece of chenille wire (note: work over beg
strand so you don't have to sew in); leave about a
half inch unworked (20–25 sts). Do not finish off.
Carefully insert stem from left to right through holes
at the uppermost part of body (near point) behind
the front stitches. This would be the space where
there is no shell. Take care that the stitches don't get
caught as you're pulling it through. Holding stem
up, above the body, bend the two pieces together and
wrap ends around one another so they won't move as
you crochet over them. Be sure stitches sit up around
the outside, not the inside. Finish covering the unworked portion with sc stitches. When complete, sew
ends in, then turn so that the join is at the bottom,
where it will be hidden by the head.

ASSEMBLY

Glue head (right side in front) to top of body. Glue
body to wings (right side in front), making sure the
halo is above the head and the chenille stem on
the wings is at the top. Glue the red heart sequin
over the angel's "heart."

SANDRA PETIT

Sandra Petit grew up in southern Louisiana and lives in the New Orleans area with her husband of more than twenty years and her two teenage, homeschooled children. She believes God's timing is always perfect and welcomes the opportunity He has given her to share her faith through tales of romance. She prays that each of her readers will experience the love and joy of having Jesus in their lives and invites you to visit her Web site at www.sandrapetit.com.

An Angel for Everyone

Gail Sattler

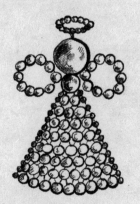

Chapter 1

Trent Johnson tipped back his head and smiled.

"Hey, Trent. It looks great."

He nodded to acknowledge Pastor Mark without looking at him. His smile dropped as he pressed his fists into the small of his back and stretched. "Yeah. It's even better than he said it would be. And bigger, too."

Beside him, Pastor Mark sighed. The shuffle of winter outerwear told Trent that his pastor also felt the effects of what they'd done. "I can't believe we got it in here. This is the biggest Christmas tree I've ever seen. Indoors, anyway."

Again, Trent stretched his sore back, this time twisting from side to side to get the kinks out. The tree was so heavy that it had taken three men to drag it inside, and that was only after they bound the branches tighter because it was too full to get inside the double doors of the church building. "I know. But it will be easier to get it out, because we'll be able to cut off some branches."

Pastor Mark groaned. "It's not even decorated yet, and you're already talking about destroying it."

Trent looked up to the twelve-foot ceiling, only three inches above the top of their newly acquired Christmas tree. "Actually, I was a little worried we were going to have to trim it to get it to stand upright. I have my chain saw in my car." He craned his neck back again. "How long do you think it will take to decorate?"

"I have no idea. All I know is that Stephanie promised that the committee would have the tree and the room done in time for the banquet Saturday night."

Trent checked his watch. It had taken longer than expected to get the tree upright, and then he and Pastor Mark had to get it properly secured and positioned so it would be ready for the decorating committee's arrival, which was supposed to be fifteen minutes ago.

Pastor Mark smiled as he again looked upward. "The tree really looks great, Trent. You really outdid yourself this year. For a while, though, I didn't think we—"

The door creaked open, and the clacking of running footsteps echoed in the large, empty room. "I'm sorry I'm late! I'm so glad someone is still here!"

Trent spun around to face the newcomer. As soon as he saw the face of his neighbor, he froze.

Kim Warner had lived next door to him since before he could remember. Years ago, when they were both in high school, she'd had a cute crush on him, which wouldn't have been bad except that she'd been born and raised in a Christian home and he hadn't. She'd always been a good girl and a good person. He hadn't been so good, and while her attention had been tremendously flattering at the time, now that he was older and had accepted Christ, he was glad he hadn't taken advantage of her. Now at least he could look her in the face without guilt.

He'd always thought she was nice, and lately he'd been starting to think about finding the woman who would be right for him—but that woman wasn't Kim. A few of the other men from the college and career group had their eyes on her. When she decided to settle down and get married, she deserved to spend her life with someone of the same caliber, and that person wasn't him.

He forced himself to smile. "Hey, Kim. It's good

to see you. But it looks like you're not the only one on the decorating committee who's late."

Kim Warner gave him a nervous smile, and with the smile, her cheeks flushed. "I have some bad news. When I arrived at Gary's house to pick him up, I found out that the reason he wasn't in church yesterday was because he's in the hospital with appendicitis. He's okay now, but he's not going to be in any shape to be decorating any tree, the church's or his own. Yesterday Sylvia had to go out of town on an unexpected business trip, so I knew she couldn't do it."

Trent frowned. "But what about Ellen? I was talking to her last week, and she told me she was going to help with the decorating, as much as she could anyway."

Pastor Mark smiled. "She had her baby yesterday, a month early, remember?" His smile dropped. "But no one told me about Gary, and I was at the hospital without seeing him."

"He was in emergency surgery Sunday afternoon," Kim said, "so you wouldn't have been able to see him even if you had known."

Pastor Mark pulled out his organizer and tapped in a note to himself. "I'll call in the morning and see when I can pay him a visit." His hand froze in midair before he completed his entry. "If the committee is down by three people, then that means. . ." He let his voice trail off.

Kim nodded. "That means I'm the only one who is healthy and available."

Trent felt his pastor's gaze upon him, heating up the skin on his face. "Surely there's someone else who can help?"

But even as Trent asked, he already knew Kim's answer before she said it.

"No. This year we want the banquet to be an outreach to the community and not just for our own church members. Everything is being provided by volunteers, including some of the food, in order to keep costs down. I think everyone in the church is doing something, even if it's just folding napkins. I already tried to find someone else to fill in for Sylvia, then Ellen. There's no one left. Everyone else who can do something is already busy on another committee."

Trent was on another committee, but it was a committee of one. He had volunteered to acquire a tree, and he had. It had taken weeks of hunting, but he'd found a good, healthy tree that a farmer was going to cut down in order to expand one of his outbuildings. After much negotiation, it was only when Trent offered to buy the man and his family tickets to the banquet that the farmer finally agreed to cut it down carefully, in one piece. Then, to Trent's surprise and delight, the farmer not only gave the tree to the church free of charge but even helped deliver it and haul it inside.

Trent personally didn't care if the decorating would be sparse. He didn't even put up a tree at home, because he lived alone. His mother gave him a wreath every year to hang on his front door, and that was good enough. But the congregation expected traditional decorations, and the farmer would expect his donation to look good.

Trent looked back up at the huge, plain pine tree, then down at Kim. If he didn't volunteer, Kim would have to do everything herself, and that wouldn't be a good thing. He didn't want her to risk injury by working alone. Not only would no one be there to hold the ladder, but even if she made it to the top rung, she was still too short to reach the top of the tree—not to mention she would have to decorate the room all by herself.

But he'd already sacrificed too much time finding the tree. His Christmas shopping wasn't done, and he hadn't sent out a single Christmas card or e-mail. He also hadn't taken his mother out for dinner, something he did every year during the holiday season.

But if he didn't help Kim, no one would. For all she'd done for him—and everyone else—she didn't deserve to be left high and dry.

He gritted his teeth, then forced himself to smile. "I think I can find the time to help decorate the tree with you."

Kim's eyes widened. "You would?" she gasped.

Her surprise almost hurt his pride. "Of course."

"Are you sure you have time?"

"Yes." *No.* But sometimes there were choices to be made, and this was one he had to make. Kim was one of the main reasons he'd started attending church and then came to know Jesus as his Lord and Savior. She always sacrificed her time to help others learn about Jesus, and since the banquet was supposed to be an outreach to the community, this was a good time to follow her example.

If he had to justify the time, he told himself that if he had to be on any more committees, this one was best because he lived next door to the only other committee member. For the work they needed to do at the church, they would drive together, so there would be no impatient waiting; and for anything they had to figure out together, once he had his coat and boots on, he could be at Kim's door in twenty seconds.

Also, years ago, she'd hurt herself because of him, and he'd always felt like he owed her something. Now he could finally pay her back.

"Wow." Her eyes lit up as her voice trailed off.

All Trent could do was stare. He hadn't seen Christmas lights as beautiful as Kim's sparkling green eyes. He wondered why he hadn't noticed before.

"That's wonderful!" she chirped as she held out a brightly colored gift bag. "I brought the first thing to put under the tree, and that's the party favors I made to give to everyone."

Pastor Mark cleared his throat. "It looks like you two have everything under control. If I don't talk to either of you before then, I'll see you Saturday at the banquet. Have fun."

They both waved as Pastor Mark made his way out and the door clicked closed behind him.

Chapter 2

Kim Warner tried to control the frantic beating of her heart.

Pastor Mark's words echoed through her head.

"Have fun," he'd said.

She didn't know if she could have fun with Trent. She'd lived next door to him nearly all her life. During her teenage years, she'd developed the most insane crush on him. For a while she thought she'd grown out of it, but when he started attending her church, those old feelings came back; and the reasons she'd fallen in love with him in the first place hit her tenfold. Now, as an adult, those same qualities, plus the fact that he'd become a believer, made her love him even more.

But to him, all she would ever be was the ditzy sixteen-year-old who'd built a ramshackle tree house just so she could talk to him over the fence one summer, then had broken her arm when the structure collapsed with her in it. He hadn't ever taken her seriously before that, and he certainly hadn't afterward, not even as an adult.

Trent looked at her. She couldn't read his expression, but he didn't look exactly eager to help.

"You don't have to do this, you know. It will just take longer, but I'm sure I can do it alone." If she worked every evening until Saturday, up to the time everyone who was bringing food started to arrive.

He turned his head and fixed all his attention on the top of the tall tree. "No. I happen to know from a good source that your sense of balance gets exponentially worse the higher you go. I could never forgive myself if something happened to you. Especially if you were here all alone just because you were being stubborn."

"I've overcome my fear of heights."

His face tightened. "I think the jury's out on that one. I remember vividly the day you developed that fear of heights, and for good reason. Let's get started. Saturday will be here before we both know what hit us."

She knew what he was referring to. Memories of that day came back in a rush, none of them good. Her parents hadn't been home, nor had his. She didn't know what had made the day worse—the mind-numbing pain of breaking her arm in three places and trying to tell him she wasn't hurt too badly, or the terror of being in the car with him as he drove like a madman to the hospital, less than a week after he had gotten his driver's license.

Now she worked in a nice safe office on the first floor, and the most innovative projects she made were knitted or crocheted crafts, done while she was sitting safely on the couch in her living room. In reasonable light.

She stared up into his face. "Trent? Are you okay? You seem a little pale."

"I think I've been standing inside too long with my coat on." He shrugged it off and tossed it against the wall, and when he did so, some of his color started to come back.

"But. . ." Her voice trailed off as she looked closely into his face. She'd always thought that being too warm would make a person flushed, not pale, making her wonder if perhaps he was coming down with the flu.

Before she could think about it anymore, he extended one open palm. "As I recall, the decorations are in the attic. If you'll give me the key, I'll get them for you. I know you can't reach that high."

Without giving her a chance to respond, he plucked the key from her fingers, turned, and left the sanctuary, which also served as the banquet hall and activity room, depending on the arrangement of chairs and tables that day.

She followed him down the hall and up the flight of stairs leading to the storage area. He reached up and unlocked the trapdoor in the low ceiling, then pulled it open and tugged the rope to bring down a folded-up, hanging metal ladder.

He turned around. "Stay here, with both feet on the floor. I'll hand you down the boxes of Christmas decorations," he said, then climbed up into the storage area.

His footsteps echoed down from the ceiling. She heard the grumble of words she couldn't make out, and then the footsteps above her stopped.

Kim shuffled closer to the opening, rested her hand on the ladder, climbed up one step, and froze, not daring to raise her foot off the thin rung. The slight sway made her nauseous. She struggled to push the sensation away, tipped back her head, and called up through the opening above her. "Trent? Are you okay up there? What's wrong?"

The tips of his boots appeared in the opening, and way above his boots, his head appeared as he leaned slightly forward and looked down. "Do you remember in the spring, when those squirrels got into the attic?"

Kim remembered it well. One Sunday morning the entire congregation had quieted for prayer, and suddenly the mad scampering of many tiny feet had echoed through the sanctuary. Pastor Mark had prayed for the animals to find another home, and then someone had gone into the attic to scare them all away while a few of the men from the congregation patched up the hole where they'd come in.

"Don't tell me they're still up there," she called upward.

"Not at the moment, but I can certainly see where they've been. It looks like they came back for a while—or something else got in here after they were gone. There are holes in all of the boxes. Stuff is falling out, and some of the boxes fell over, and everything inside is broken. And some stuff, well, it looks like they were either nesting or had babies in there for a while, because the contents are, well, uh. . .not very clean."

"Is anything still good?"

"I don't know. I want you to be prepared for what you see, and please, stand back so you don't get hit with any debris."

When they had everything down, Kim almost cried. Most of the garland was either crushed or soiled in some place, and when one part of the length was ruined, the whole piece was ruined. One of the boxes that had fallen over contained the glass ornaments, which now were all broken. Some of the ornaments were made of either wood or a flour-and-water mixture, and most of those were chewed. Many had been made by Sunday school classes over the years and were made of paper and macaroni. Most of those were either eaten or shredded, and those that weren't shredded smelled funny.

Trent ran his fingers through his hair. "What are we going to do? We were supposed to start today."

Kim straightened and rested her fists on her hips as she scanned all the boxes around them. "I don't know why, but I have lots of money left over in my budget for making the gifts for the guests. I suppose I could use it to buy new decorations. Although usually we buy that kind of stuff after Christmas, when it's half price."

Trent checked his watch. "It's actually getting

pretty late. Is there anything in that bag we can decorate with? I hate to waste the night."

"Not really." Kim sighed. The only thing she'd brought were the gifts meant for the banquet guests.

They pushed the ruined boxes to the side and returned to the multipurpose room, where the gift bag she'd brought sat next to the tree. She pushed the tissue paper aside, reached inside, and pulled out one of her creations. "This is all I brought."

"What is it?"

Her cheeks burned. "It's a beaded angel, silly. I made a bunch of them for the guests. We're going to give one away to everyone who comes, as a memento of the evening."

"But it's so small."

"It's not supposed to be big. I think they're cute, and they turned out just like they were supposed to."

"I guess. I suppose they are cute. You did a nice job." He smiled, then reached into the bag, but he froze as his fingers touched the pile of angels inside. "If those are supposed to be mementos for the guests, there aren't many in here."

"I made the exact number Stephanie told me to."

"What are you talking about?"

Kim dug through her purse and pulled out the

crinkled piece of paper that Stephanie, the church secretary, had given her. "Here's what she said." Kim began to read. "'This year we're going to give one small gift to everyone who attends the banquet, instead of larger gifts to only a few lucky winners. We decided on these beaded angels. Here are the instructions and the money for your supplies. Just bring back receipts and the change. We'll need you to make thirty.'"

Kim lowered the note. "It's really strange that she made such a mistake with the money. I had way too much, but she didn't say to buy anything else." Just in case she missed something, Kim flipped the paper over, but as it had been every other time she checked, it was blank.

Trent crossed his arms over his chest. "Something isn't right. Stephanie is usually meticulously accurate, especially with money. Didn't you think that was a little odd? Also, don't you think thirty is a strange number to ask for?"

Kim shrugged her shoulders. "Not really. I'm sure she has other people making them, too. I just don't understand how she could make such a mistake with the money."

Trent sucked in a deep breath. "I know how many tickets we had printed, and they're all gone. Can I see

132

that note?" His brows knotted as he reread it. "This note is really badly written."

"Yes. When she was writing it, her pen was running out of ink and she couldn't find another one. I had to go. I was already late. That's the best she could do. But it's okay. I know what it says."

"I have a bad feeling." Trent ran his fingers over the number. "Last I heard, we're expecting over 270 people, and that was a couple of weeks ago. Can you see how the pen made an indent on the paper? I don't think she was scribbling to make the pen write. I think she only wrote the actual number down. The pen actually did spit out a bit of ink. The way I see it, this doesn't say thirty; it says three hundred."

"But that's not possible. How could she think I had time to make three hundred beaded angels?"

"Maybe she assumed you'd ask other people for help if you needed it. Just how much money do you have left over?"

If Kim didn't feel sick enough after her attempt to go up the ladder, she felt doubly so now.

Without a word, she pulled her calculator out of her purse and refigured the amount of money needed for the new number of angels.

The final total bought her near the edge of having

to run to the washroom. Her voice came out in a rough croak. "If I was supposed to make three hundred, that leaves me with under five dollars in change. I think you're right."

She looked up at Trent. "Once I got good at making these angels, each one took me twenty minutes to do." She frantically began punching more numbers into the calculator. "Not including the shopping time, it will take me fifty-four hundred minutes to make the rest. That's. . .ninety hours. . . ." Her voice totally failed. She punched in a few more numbers. "That's nearly four whole days, if I don't eat, sleep, or go to work. But I can't even start until after I go shopping to buy the rest of the supplies, and we need the angels finished for supper time on Saturday. Today is already Monday. That's only five days away."

Trent laughed weakly. "I said earlier that Saturday was going to hit us before we knew it. Now it feels really creepy, having said that."

She turned and looked blankly at the plain, oversized tree. "And $4.57 isn't going to buy many decorations. Our budget for the banquet was already stretched to the max. There isn't any money left, and I certainly don't have enough time to make all those angels.

"We have to decorate. What am I going to do?"

Chapter 3

Every second felt like an hour while Kim waited for Trent to reply. Not that she really expected an answer. She knew he wouldn't have one. If she had to, she knew she could buy some new decorations for the church and put them on her credit card, then work it out with Stephanie later.

But she couldn't put the time it would take to make 270 angels on her credit card.

She looked again at the note. It now seemed obvious that she should have known she would need more than thirty angels, but as usual, hindsight was twenty-twenty. This time she felt even more foolish than when she fell out of the tree house. At least then she could use youth, a complete lack of mechanical aptitude, unbridled enthusiasm, and an extreme case of puppy love as an excuse.

Now none of those applied, except, in a way, the puppy love—although as an adult, she really didn't believe in puppy love anymore. But she did believe in love. Yet no matter what she did, either in the neighborhood or at church, Trent never seemed to notice her.

She looked up at Trent.

She couldn't remember a time when she didn't like him. For years, ever since she was fifteen, which was ten years ago, she'd gone through various stages of trying to get him to notice her, but he never did. Many times she'd given up and gone on with her life. Then, sooner or later, her feelings for him came back and she found herself in the same position. And every time was the same as the time before. He simply never noticed her. Now, after all these years, she finally had his undivided attention.

She was sure that God truly did have a sense of humor. The only other time she'd had his full attention was when she was writhing in pain on the ground. Now, ten years later, instead of physical pain, this time it was mental. This wasn't the way it was supposed to happen.

"It's more than obvious that I'm going to have to

call for reinforcements. Do you have any idea who has a few hours they can spare before the banquet?"

He gave a short, humorless laugh. "A few hours?"

"At this point I have to tell myself that every little bit counts. Otherwise I should just give up."

Trent shook his head. "No, I didn't mean it that way. You're right, of course. Are these things hard to do?"

"No. They're actually pretty easy. Stephanie gave me really simple instructions to follow."

"Do you think I could do it? If so, you have your first volunteer."

"Really?"

"Unless you think I'm completely incapable."

Her cheeks flamed. She'd always admired his intelligence, but more than that, he had an innovative way of thinking that she found just as fascinating now as she had ten years ago.

"Of course I don't think that. I just know how busy you are, with night school and everything."

"I have an assignment that has to be in after the Christmas break, but I think I can spare a few days. And it will only be a few days. So don't worry about it. I'm nearly done anyway, so it will be easy to make up the lost time. I can just take my books to work and read on my lunch breaks."

Kim shook her head. "I don't know how you do it."

"I have to support myself, so I have to work. That leaves night school. It will just take a little longer to get my certificate. After that I can go for my apprenticeship, and onward I'll go."

Kim was happy with her office job, even though she knew she didn't have much opportunity for advancement. She was happy, most days at least, and the office was on ground level.

She turned away from Trent and focused on the huge tree in the corner. "Actually, if you help, that should really make a difference. I think I can probably get a day off work, and if so, I'll see if I can get the ladies' coffee group that meets Wednesday mornings to do some. If everyone can do even four or five each over the two-hour meeting, that will make a big difference."

"That's a good start."

"I feel better already. I think this is doable. And now, about the decorations." She glanced around the room. "A little garland would go a long way if we only looped it around the walls. But the tree is another matter. It's huge, so it's going to take a lot to fill it. Wait a minute. . . ." Her voice trailed off as images started to form in her mind, like snow gently falling down, landing on the tree, and taking shape, transforming from a blur into a surreal picture—almost real enough to see.

"I have an idea!" she exclaimed as she spun around to face Trent.

At the sudden volume of her voice, Trent flinched and stiffened.

Again Kim spun around and stepped closer to the tree. She reached out and fingered one of the branches, then tipped her head back to see all the way to the top.

"We can decorate the tree with the three hundred beaded angels! Can you imagine how pretty that will be? Picture it. The deep green of the tree, the shimmering white beads of the angels, the rich gold of the halos, and the delicate fluff of the white lace wings. . . . It's going to be gorgeous! All I have to do is add a gold loop on the back to hang them, and they'll be perfect! Then we can pick them off one at a time and give them away to everyone as they leave. The tree might be left bare, but it won't matter, because the banquet will be over."

"I'm not so sure that's what Stephanie had in mind, but the idea has potential."

Before he had a chance to turn down the idea, Kim quickly balanced one of the small beaded angels on one of the branches. "See?" she asked as she stepped back. "Doesn't that look nice?"

Trent didn't move from where he stood. "Actually, you're right. The white on the dark green does look good."

"I've got a gold star at home that's too big for my small artificial tree. I can bring it here, and the church can use it." She clasped her hands in front of her chest and spun around on her toes. "I think it will be perfect! I feel so much better now. I bet I can even get one big spool of gold thread with the money I have left. I could even stay within my budget."

"Maybe, but that doesn't change the fact that we have an awful lot to do before it's going to happen."

Kim checked her watch. She tried not to get too excited at his automatic *we*, which meant that they were in this together. "The stores are open late every night until Christmas, including weekends—the craft store, too. If I can make it before they close, I might be able to start tonight. At this point, every twenty minutes is one more angel. Bye!"

She began running to the door but stopped after a few steps and turned around. "I almost forgot. We left the wrecked decorations in the hallway. We can't leave them like that."

Trent waved one hand in the air. "I can pick through the boxes and take out anything salvageable. You go. I'll be fine."

With a quick nod, Kim turned and ran out the door.

She did manage to make it to the craft store without a speeding ticket just as the clerk locked the door.

Kim held up the directions and pressed the paper to the glass. "Please, you've got to let me in!" she called out loudly enough to be heard through the glass. "I know what I need, and I have to get all this stuff tonight!"

The clerk looked up to the clock, then at the directions. She sighed and pulled open the door so Kim could enter.

"I shouldn't be doing this. I'm supposed to stand here and let people out and tell anyone new to come back tomorrow. But if you promise you'll be fast, you can get what you need."

"Thank you!" Kim said without stopping.

Since she had already purchased the same materials a few weeks ago, she knew exactly where to find what she needed. She threw everything into a basket and hurried to the checkout, very proud of herself that she wasn't the last person in line.

She said a special thank-you to the woman who was still posted at the door and hurried to her car. But before she went home for the night, Kim had one more stop to make.

The coffee shop. She needed a large mocha grande. Maybe two. It was going to be a long night.

Chapter 4

Trent slowed his car, hit the switch for the remote garage-door opener, and pulled into the driveway to wait for the door to open.

While he waited, he studied Kim's closed living room curtains.

He couldn't see her, but he knew what she was doing.

Trent drove into the garage, but instead of going inside the house, he stared through the opening of the still-raised garage door.

Despite the time, he knew Kim would be at it for many, many more hours.

He sighed, tensed, pushed the button to close the door, then ran the length of the garage, ducking under the door as it descended. Once outside, he straightened. He waited only until the bottom of the door touched the ground, then, patting his keys in his pocket, he walked next door and knocked.

"Trent? What are you doing here? Don't you have to get up early for work in the morning?"

He forced himself to smile. "Yes. Don't you?"

"Well, yes. But I, uh. . ." Her voice trailed off.

"You weren't thinking of pulling off an all-nighter already, were you? There's no need to panic, at least not yet. Is there?"

She ran her fingers through her hair, something Trent knew Kim only did when she was stressed.

"I figured it all out in the car," she muttered. "Between my coffee breaks and my lunch break, I can make three angels every day at work. If I work at these until midnight, then I can do nineteen or twenty each evening, and if I get up early, I can probably get one done while I'm eating breakfast. That way I can probably do twenty-four per day." She sucked in a deep breath and went on. "If I start tomorrow"—she started counting on her fingers—"and if I get Wednesday off, I can do another twenty. If you help me for three hours a night, plus what I figure the ladies' group could do Wednesday morning, and then what we could do Saturday before the banquet, that makes 282." Her

144

eyes brightened, and she actually started to smile. "So if I can do eighteen tonight, even though I'm starting a few hours late, then it really is possible. I'll just stay up until I'm done."

Trent sighed. Maybe panic had started to set in. The way she was tossing around numbers did nothing to help calm her. The fact that she had memorized all the figures told him that despite her words, she wasn't as sure as she tried to appear that she could actually do it.

Now it was Trent's turn to run his fingers through his hair. "May I come in?"

Her cheeks darkened. "Of course. Would you like some coffee?"

As they walked into the kitchen, he saw two large, empty paper cups from the local coffee shop, in addition to a pot of coffee on the counter that was down by half.

He shook his head. He thought he'd detected a tremor in her hands. A strange feeling rolled through his stomach, making him wonder if it had been too long since he'd last eaten.

Trent extended one hand toward the counter. "This isn't the solution, you know. It's not worth killing yourself. The banquet isn't going to be a failure just because you don't get all the angels done."

"That's not the point. I said I would do this, and I'm only as good as my word. As it is, the decorations have been ruined. I can't let this be ruined, too."

"That wasn't your fault."

"No, but that's not the point. Everything has to look festive and cheerful. It's Christmas."

Trent shoved his hands into his pockets. He didn't want a pack of wayward rodents to spoil anything in Kim's Christmas. "I was thinking that I'd buy some new decorations on the way home from work tomorrow. That will at least solve the decorating crisis. But since you've got it all figured out, if I can help you tonight, that's only a dozen each. I think we can do that and still get to bed at a decent hour. We both have to get up for work tomorrow."

Kim smiled, which suddenly made the concept of staying up until the wee hours and going to work with not enough sleep seem like not so much of a sacrifice.

"Are you sure you want to stay?"

"If I wasn't sure, I wouldn't have asked. Show me what to do."

Her smile widened.

Trent forced himself to keep smiling, He'd never

done such a thing before, and he really didn't know what he was doing. However, he didn't want anything to ruin the Christmas season for Kim. She was already stressed, and he couldn't see her getting any calmer until the angel situation was at least under control. If this was what it would take to make this Christmas a good one for her, then he would do it.

He walked to the kitchen table, which was strewn with bags of beads, ribbon, a spool of gold wire, and a pile of clipped lace pieces. Another pile to the side showed she'd already completed three angels that evening.

Trent glanced at the clock. If he got to bed at 1:00 a.m., then they had another three hours, which meant they could make nine angels each. It was a bit short of what she needed, but it was a start, and much better than if she had to work alone.

"I'm going to warn you; it took me longer to do the first one, so don't feel discouraged. It only took a couple, and I was up to the top speed of twenty minutes each."

He rubbed his hands together. "Then let's get started."

He copied her movement for movement as she strung the first row of beads on the wire, then double strung each subsequent row to give it the right shape.

"This isn't so hard," he said as he tightened everything up when he finished the single bead at the top of the triangle, then checked the clock.

"That was the easy part. Now we do the arms. The smaller beads are harder to do."

Trent picked up a bead and was about to string it when the phone rang.

Kim's eyebrows quirked. "I wonder who would be phoning at this hour. I hope nothing is wrong."

While she hurried to the phone, Trent closed one eye and poked the wire at the hole.

And missed.

After a few more attempts, he took a deep breath, held it, and finally poked the wire through. No longer fully concentrating on the tiny hole, Kim's laughter registered in his mind. He wasn't going to listen to her conversation, but the small laugh indicated that whoever was calling didn't have bad news. He hadn't realized that he'd become tense until he felt himself sag at the confirmation that nothing was wrong.

Trent picked up a second bead, held his breath, and poked the wire at it until he finally got it through, too.

This time, as he let his concentration on the bead lapse, he couldn't help hearing Kim tell the caller that she really had to get off the phone. Yet instead of hanging up, she continued to protest, indicating that the caller wasn't giving up easily, despite the late hour.

Trent picked up the third bead and held his breath, but this time he froze with the wire in midair, still pointed at the microscopic opening.

Each arm contained seven beads, and the halo contained ten beads of the same size. If it was taking him this long to string the smaller beads, his angels were going to take a lot longer than twenty minutes each.

Briefly he considered taking some beads to work and doing them there on his breaks. In order to do what he'd promised, Kim's frantic figuring had counted on him producing a certain number a day, and at this rate, he was going to be lucky to make one.

Suddenly he understood why it was so important to Kim to get the required amount done for the banquet. He was feeling the same way about getting the number done for her that she'd counted on from him.

"Sorry I took so long. That was Katie from work. I can't believe she'd be calling at this hour; but she needs a ride to work in the morning, and she asked if I could pick her up. . . ." Kim's voice trailed off. "What are you doing?"

"Yes!" Trent muttered between his lips as he got

the third bead on the wire.

He lowered it to the table, being very careful to place it so there was no chance of his hard work coming off.

"I'm almost done with one arm."

She narrowed her eyes and leaned down to inspect his handiwork. "You're not almost done. You've got. . . three beads. . . ." Her voice trailed off again.

He sighed. "You were right. It's harder than it looks. I don't know if I can do this. Or if I can, I can't do it as fast as you're going to need." He glanced at the clock. "I don't know how you can get one finished in only twenty minutes."

"You weren't trying to thread the beads, were you? For the smaller beads, you leave them on the table, brace them with your finger, and then poke the wire through, like this."

In seconds flat, she had all six beads for her angel's one arm on the wire. He could see how doing it her way made sense. He hadn't considered there could be more than one way to string a bead.

She looked up at the clock. "We still have lots of time, but we should get back at it."

Her graciousness in the face of his foolishness impressed him.

He watched, then copied Kim's method, agreeing without saying so that she was right. It took him as long to do the arms as it did the rest of the body, but he did get them done.

It was a relief to add the head, which was the easiest bead to do, being the largest.

"Now we do the halo."

Trent sighed. "I know. With the same size beads as the arms. Maybe I will take you up on that coffee. But I do have to set a limit. I should be out of here at one o'clock, or I'm going to be useless at work tomorrow."

"That's actually longer than I expected you to stay. I'll set the timer. We can meet back here after supper tomorrow to do more."

Her smile widened. Something in Trent's stomach went haywire, making him wonder if he'd somehow passed his limit on the amount of coffee he'd consumed.

"We can do this," she said, and as she smiled, cute little crinkles appeared at the corners of her eyes. "Now I know that everything is going to be okay."

Chapter 5

I t's not going to work." Kim's voice cracked over the phone.

Trent froze.

They'd recalculated the time they needed because Kim had forgotten to include how long it would take to decorate the tree before the guests arrived on Saturday. But because he'd agreed to go to her house straight from work, and he could make eighteen per day instead of twelve, it was still reasonably possible that they could indeed meet their goal.

However, it was Wednesday afternoon, and for some reason, she was calling him at work.

"I don't understand," Trent mumbled in response.

"First of all, not as many ladies came to the coffee group session as expected. Most of the ladies said they'd give the angels a try, but just as I started to show everyone what to do, a guest speaker arrived. She got her dates mixed up and thought she was supposed to come this week, but she was scheduled for next week. With everything so mixed up, some ladies didn't even make one. Those ladies who did figure it out were listening to the speaker at the same time they were making angels, so they didn't get as many done as if they had just been sitting there concentrating exclusively on the angels."

"I'm afraid to ask."

"I'd counted on the ladies' group doing over a hundred, but they only made fourteen; and I've got six in varying stages to finish up."

Trent squeezed his eyes shut. Even if he took a day off work, which he couldn't this time of year, he could never make up that kind of shortage. And time was running out.

"But that's not all. When I got home, a bunch of the beads were missing. I phoned Stephanie at the church, but she couldn't find them anywhere. A number of the ladies brought their preschool-age children, and I have a bad feeling that some of the young children thought the gold beads were pretty and took some home. Some of the white ones are missing, too. I have to count what's left, and then I have to go shopping again."

Trent checked his watch. "Maybe we could go together. I still have to get some garland and see if I can find anything else at a reasonable price to decorate the walls." To say nothing of needing to do the rest of his Christmas shopping. It was probably too late to do it online. If he left the rest of his shopping until after the banquet, that left him less than a week before Christmas to get it done. He thought he'd learned his lesson from last year not to let it go so late, but now he was finding himself in the same position. That it wasn't his fault this year wasn't going to make any difference.

A silence hung over the line. Trent waited, not so patiently, until Kim finally spoke.

"It sounds like you intend to pay for it. You don't have to. You're not even really on the decorating committee."

"I don't think it counts as a committee anymore, because you're now a committee of one. Besides, I already offered." If he didn't insist on paying, he knew that she would. He doubted she was going to ask Stephanie for the money. He didn't usually feel this way, but something inside him wanted to be gallant.

Even though it was for the church and not directly for Kim, it was still important to her. "What time can I pick you up?"

Another pause hung on the line. "It doesn't matter. I'm at home now, making more angels."

"Then I'll pick you up at five thirty. We can run out, get what we need, then grab a couple of burgers on the way home and eat while we work."

He waited for her to say something, but she didn't.

Trent cleared his throat. "I think that's probably the most efficient way to get everything done the fastest."

"I think it's more efficient for one of us to stay home and the other to shop."

"I'm going to be the one stringing the garland, so I have to buy that, and I think you'd best buy the beads. I don't want to get the wrong thing. If the craft shop has garland, it will be a fast trip."

"Okay. I'll see you later."

Trent returned to his current project, but his thoughts kept wandering back to Kim.

He'd known her almost all his life, but he'd never really paid attention to her until the day she broke her arm while she was trying to build that ridiculous ramshackle tree house by herself. After she healed, he'd considered asking her out for a date, but his friends had laughed at him, telling him he would never have any fun going out with someone so religious. Actually, he'd always respected her for her faith, even before he became a Christian himself. She always did the right thing and never hurt anyone, except herself, and that was by accident. Most important, if he'd been more like her, sooner, then his whole life would have been different. But it was too late now. If the best he could do was take her shopping and sit and do crafts, then that was the way it had to be. As the saying went, he had made his own bed, and now he had to lie in it.

A day had never dragged on so long, until the time he pulled up in front of Kim's house. Just as he turned off the ignition, she ran out the door. He barely had time to open the door locks before she reached the door and slid inside the car.

"Let's go. I phoned ahead, and they have the beads put aside for me. The lady at the store said they also have lots of nice garland left, so this will be a quick trip."

Trent's mouth opened, but no sound came out. He hadn't wanted it to be a quick trip, even though he knew it should be.

Despite his earlier words, he also didn't want to rush, and he didn't want to get dinner from the drive-through. He wanted to go someplace they could sit down and talk without having a looming project distracting them, even though he knew that was wrong. That situation would be too close to a date, and he couldn't allow her to think such a thing was possible. Dating at their age meant that the possibility of marriage existed, and for him, that wasn't an option with Kim.

He cleared his throat. "I changed my mind. I want to go check out the mall. They have a better selection, and they might have some cheap decorations, too."

He pulled away from the curb and headed in the direction of the craft store. Even though she wasn't speaking, he could feel Kim looking at him.

"We don't have time for that. You're not taking this seriously, are you?" she asked in a voice so quiet she was almost whispering.

The hurt in her voice made his empty stomach clench painfully. "No, it's not that at all. It's just that. . ." His voice trailed off. He really didn't care about the mall, but once they were there, he thought he might be able to convince her to take some time off and go to a restaurant with him for dinner, even if it was just the family restaurant at the crowded mall. After the banquet was over, everything would be back to the way it was before, the way it had been for the last five years, which involved nothing more than exchanging a friendly wave over the backyard fence. The only other occasions he spent significant time with her occurred in the safety net of a group situation at the college and career events at church. For once, he wanted a taste of what he couldn't have, but that was wrong. "I suppose you're right. I'm sorry. I'm sure the garland at the craft store will be fine."

"The lady at the store told me she has the perfect thing, and she told me where to find it. We just have to hurry."

"Please don't worry so much. Even with this little setback, I'm sure we'll be able to make everything we need. I was thinking—you're doing some angels on your breaks at work. I can do the same."

"You'd do that? Don't you think you'll feel silly?"

Trent grinned, picturing in his mind the reactions he was bound to witness. "Nah. Actually, once I start, I know that initially I'll attract some attention. It's not often you see a man doing this kind of thing. But that's not a bad thing. I bet a few of the ladies would be more than happy to help me. We could even get quite a few extra done that way."

"What a great idea! Maybe I'll ask some of my

friends at work if they could do one on their lunch break with me. At this point, every angel done is one more angel."

When they reached the small strip mall where the craft store was, Kim helped find a parking spot. As they walked toward the store, Trent noticed a number of men waiting in their cars, some with children but also a few alone.

Once he actually stepped inside the craft store, he discovered why. He'd never been inside a craft store in his life, and being inside, he felt even more out of place than he thought he would.

The first thing he saw was row upon row of flowers, lace, ribbon, frilly hearts, and other pretty things that most men wouldn't be caught dead with. He followed Kim to the left, where they passed a rack called "tools," which contained a variety of tiny little glue guns, many of them pink and other feminine colors, with glue sticks so small they would be used up in one press of the trigger if he were using his own glue gun in the garage. There were scissors of all shapes and sizes, little knives, racks and holders, and loops of wire.

There wasn't a hammer or a set of real pliers to be seen.

Kim turned into the next row. He followed her

past countless skeins of thread of every shade of every color of the rainbow, and then some, along with little packages of cloth and a huge rack of pattern books. Those he could understand. His mother had done embroidery when he was a child.

When they reached the end of the aisle, he saw a display along the back wall of the store that contained everything from fabric to ribbon to plastic shapes, in obvious Christmas colors and patterns.

She turned to him. "They put the Christmas things in the back to make everyone walk through the entire store first, so hopefully they'll buy more than just what they came for."

"I suppose that's a common marketing ploy." He looked on the top shelf where there were, as promised, reels of garland. It looked a little different from the stuff he saw in the department store, but it was still garland.

"Those are really large spools. I've never seen it sold like this before."

"You buy it by the length. How much do you need?"

He pulled the envelope for his phone bill out of his back pocket, on which he'd written the dimensions of the room. "You won't believe this, but I calculated the exact amount I'd need, including the droops, just so I wouldn't buy too much. This is incredible. It will be cheaper to buy it this way than in precut packages." He put four of the spools in the buggy. "Where do we go now?"

"To the front. The beads are put aside for me. Let's go. The faster we get out of here, the sooner we can get back to my place and back to work."

Chapter 6

K im measured some coffee into the filter and then the water while Trent unpacked the bag containing their fast-food supper.

She'd almost thought he was going to suggest they go out to a real restaurant, but he'd only said he wanted to go to the mall.

She had no difficulty in turning down that suggestion.

But if he would have asked to take her out for dinner, that offer would have been hard to turn down, regardless of how much work she had left to do. It would have been totally irresponsible, but she couldn't say for sure that she would have said no.

But he didn't do that. As she should have expected. She couldn't show Trent how she felt about him—

how she'd felt about him for years. All that mattered was that he didn't feel the same way, and to hope for anything to happen now, after so long, was foolishness. The trouble was that now, after being so close to him for these few days, the reasons she'd been so attracted to him were the same, only now he had maturity and his faith to add to the list. She loved him now more than ever, even more than the day so many years ago that she almost killed herself trying to get closer to him.

It wasn't sensible, but she couldn't change how she felt. She didn't know if it was better or worse that she had seen so much of him since Sunday, but she supposed this was better than not seeing him at all.

She turned around and forced herself to smile. "All we have to do is wait for it to finish brewing. Let's eat. I'm starved."

"Me, too."

They paused for a word of thanks, then began to eat.

Without hesitation, Trent reached for an already-cut piece of wire and began stringing beads to make another angel. "I think pretty soon I'm going to be seeing these things in my dreams."

"I'm already dreaming about them, except my

dreams are becoming nightmares," Kim grumbled.

All Trent's movements stopped. "You shouldn't let this get to you so much. While these angels are nice to give away, it's not that important in the entire scheme of life. They're just decorations."

"I keep telling myself that," Kim mumbled as she slid the wire through the third layer of another angel body, "but this is really about a promise I made that I should be able to keep. I really had a month to make these, which would have been plenty of time. I should have realized there was something wrong when I was finished in less than a week."

"You made a mistake. It's not a big deal. We all make mistakes." Trent's voice lowered in pitch, so low she barely could make out his words. "Sometimes big ones," he muttered.

"What did you say? I barely heard you."

"Nothing," he mumbled. He pointed to the pile of lace clips without raising his head. "Can you pass me a wing?"

Kim wiped her fingers on a napkin and handed him one of the pieces, but when they both reached out at the same time, their fingers touched, nearly causing her to drop the lace. Instead of letting it go, she wrapped her fingers around his.

He froze under her touch but didn't pull away.

"What's wrong, Trent? You can tell me. We've known each other since forever. I like to think we're friends."

"It's nothing you or anyone can do anything about. What's done is done. It's not a big deal."

She waited for him to say more, but he didn't. His silence alone told her that contrary to his words, it was a big deal.

"Don't you want to talk about it?"

"No."

She waited, but he didn't continue. Indeed, his "no" really did mean no.

She thought for a few minutes, glancing up at him often as they worked together, trying to think of the best thing to say to get him to open up.

"Confession is good for the soul."

"I confessed already."

She waited, but he didn't elaborate.

As soon as the coffee was ready, she got up, poured two mugs, prepared his the way she knew he liked it, and returned to the table. "It's okay. God forgives all our mistakes."

He didn't look up as he spoke but concentrated intently on stringing the gold beads for another halo.

"That's true. I know God has forgiven me, but not everyone else has. Look, I really don't want to talk about this. Can we change the subject?"

Kim blinked. "I'm sorry."

This time he looked up and made eye contact. Her breath caught. She'd never seen such sadness and regret. His expression made her want to hug him and make it all better, but he'd made it very plain that there was nothing she could do. Even if there was, he wasn't going to allow her to do anything.

"Please don't be sorry. It's okay. I've come to terms with it. I've just had to make some choices, and life goes on. I was wondering. . . . This coffee is good, but you know what I'd really like? Have you got any hot chocolate?"

Kim rolled the chair back and stood, grateful for the blunt, if jarring, change of subject. "Yes, I do. I even have marshmallows. I can—"

The ringing of the phone cut off her words.

She answered to the sound of sniffling on the other end.

"Josie? What's wrong?"

Her best friend sniffled. "I'm so embarrassed. I hurt myself, and I have no one else to call. I slipped on the walkway and crashed backward into that old fence, and I have a sliver, and, uh, I can't sit down or it hurts. My medical plan at my new job doesn't kick in for another month, and, well, I don't have anyone else I can ask to pull it out. I can't see it properly, so I can't do it myself. Can you please come over?"

Kim squeezed her eyes shut.

"Please?" Josie sniffled for more effect.

Kim sighed. "Of course. I'll be right there."

"Thanks so much. I know you're busy, but the whole round-trip should take only an hour."

An hour. Three angels. But she couldn't leave her friend in pain.

"I'm on my way."

Kim hung up the phone, but she kept her hand on the receiver as she turned her head toward Trent. "I have to go. Josie needs me for something rather personal. It would probably be more efficient if you stayed here and kept working while I'm gone, if you don't mind. Just don't trash the place."

"But. . ." Slowly, his solemn expression broke into a grin. "That's pretty funny. Don't worry; I'll still be here, and I probably won't have moved except to make more hot chocolate."

Kim drove to Josie's home as fast as she could without getting a speeding ticket. Josie's red-rimmed eyes and the small spot of blood on her pants told Kim everything she needed to know. She knew how embarrassed her friend was, so she didn't say anything that didn't have to be said, including "bend over."

Once the splinter was removed, Josie's big hug and the fresh flood of tears told her she'd done the right thing by coming right away.

While Kim slipped her boots back on, Josie swiped her face with the back of her hand. "I don't know what to say. You wouldn't believe how much that hurt. I didn't know what I would have done without you."

"It's okay. I know what it's like to need help when you're down. Do you remember when my tree house came crashing down with me in it?"

"Do I ever. Trent rushed you to the hospital. Do you still have that cast?"

"Yes." Only because Trent had been the first to sign it.

Josie grinned. "How is Trent anyway?"

Kim focused all her attention on the zipper of her boot, which had become stuck in her sock. "He's fine. In fact, I left him at my house to come here. That's why I have to get back quickly."

She stood and turned to leave, but Josie's hand on her arm stopped her. "Hold it right there. Details.

I need details. You can't leave me hanging like that. What's he doing at your house?"

"It's not what you think. He's just helping me assemble the angels that we're giving to all the guests at the banquet at church Saturday night. While I'm on the subject, would you like to make some? I see you're not doing anything right now."

"Only because of, uh, what happened. I have to leave in ten minutes for Donna's house. We haven't finished the costumes yet. At least now I can sit to do some sewing. And then I have to stop at the supermarket on my way home. I'm glad it's open until midnight. I've got to make four dozen cookies for the banquet."

"I tried. I guess I'll see you Saturday."

Unfortunately, Josie didn't release her arm.

"Not so fast. Tell me more about Trent."

Kim almost told her friend that there was nothing to say, but there was something she wanted to ask.

"Josie, you've known Trent for a long time, too. I don't know what it is, but something is bothering him. He won't give me details, but it sounds like he's made some kind of error in judgment, and the guilt is crushing him."

"I don't know. I didn't really know him before he started coming to church three or four years ago.

You've known him way longer than I have."

"I was just wondering if you'd heard anything."

"Sorry. Nada."

Kim finally disengaged her sock from the zipper in her boot without making a hole. "I have to go back now. I'll have to find out some other way."

"Just be careful. Guys can sometimes get funny about talking about problems and stuff like that."

Kim closed the door behind her.

She wanted to think that Trent was above that kind of thing, but she really didn't know. But the more she thought about it, the more she realized that while he certainly wasn't a recluse, he also didn't go out a lot, and she seldom saw him dating other women. Even if he didn't bring his dates to his home, the grapevine at church told her more than she wanted to know about his love life, or lack thereof.

All she knew was that something was wrong, and she wanted to do something to help him, even if it drove him further away from her.

She loved him that much.

Chapter 7

Trent smiled the second he heard Kim's car pull into her driveway.

It sounded exactly the same as when he was at home listening for her, except it was slightly louder.

The motor cut, the car door slammed, and within ten seconds the front door opened.

He waited to hear, "Honey! I'm ho—ome!" but of course it never happened.

He squeezed his eyes shut. That only happened in his wildest dreams. This was very much reality.

Instead he heard, "I'm back. How many did you get done?"

"Nearly three. You weren't gone as long as you said you'd be."

"No. Traffic was really light. I think everyone is at a mall somewhere. I caught mostly green lights, and it didn't take very long to help Josie." Kim grinned. Something strange happened in Trent's stomach, only he knew he wasn't hungry. "She owes me big time for this."

Trent suspected that a lot of people owed her for a lot of favors, only Kim would never call on anyone to collect them. It simply wasn't in her nature to do so.

"I made fresh coffee while you were gone. Normally I'd say that I hoped it wouldn't keep you up, but in this case, the opposite is true."

"Smart man."

Trent felt his cheeks flush, which was ridiculous.

He cleared his throat. "We can't kill ourselves doing this, but we really are running out of time. While you were gone, I did some thinking. I don't have any other option but to take a bunch of stuff to work and see if any of the ladies, or even some of the other guys, will do some on their lunch breaks. Even if they don't finish one, that doesn't matter. Anything started is that much less that we have to do."

"I think that's a great idea. I'll do the same."

They worked in silence for a while, but Trent didn't want silence. Not that he wasn't comfortable without conversation, but he didn't want to waste this rare time of being alone with Kim, without anything on the agenda except for a common project for the mutual good of the church banquet.

"While you were on your way to Josie's, did you see that house on the corner of Maple Drive with all the Christmas lights? They had all the best-decorated houses in the area listed in the community paper last weekend."

"Yes. I saw it. It was spectacular. Actually, I'd love to take a drive around and see all the houses listed. Maybe even take some pictures. Would you like to come with me?"

He did want to, but he couldn't open a door that would be difficult to close; that's why, in the past, he hadn't done things like that. But being one in a crowd among the single young adults from the college and career group was a great safety barrier. "That would be great. I wonder if we could get Tyler to drive. He has a van that seats seven. I think it would be fun to go out for coffee and doughnuts afterward."

Kim's eyes narrowed, and she stared at him so intensely that he actually squirmed in his chair and dropped a bead.

He listened to it roll across the table, then bounce

to the floor and continue on its way.

"I meant just you and me. Something to celebrate finishing this project together."

"Oh. I just thought the more the merrier."

She sighed, obviously not happy with his suggestion, but he knew she couldn't dispute his idea.

They chatted about the goings-on around town for the Christmas season until they were both yawning. The timer in his PDA went off, signaling the time they had agreed to quit for the night.

"Just take what you think you'll need for tomorrow and leave everything else on the table. There isn't much point in packing it all away. I'll be back at these again at breakfast time. Which is only a few hours away."

He nodded, stifling another yawn, and scooped enough supplies to do a dozen angels into a small plastic bag. "I know what you mean. I might do the same," he said as he began walking to the door.

He slipped his boots on without lacing them up, but before he could open the door, Kim reached out and touched his arm, preventing him from leaving.

"What you said earlier has really been bothering me. You sounded so sad. I feel bad, not knowing that something was wrong and letting you go through it alone. That doesn't make me a very good friend."

He looked down at her hand on his arm. Such a small, delicate hand, but some kind of inner strength radiated from her as she touched him, holding him in place. He couldn't move.

Something about the way she held him, gentle but strong, asking but not begging, firm but still giving him the choice, completely did him in. He couldn't believe how his voice shook as he spoke. All these years, he'd been stoic, holding his head up high, all by himself.

All by himself.

He didn't want to be all by himself anymore, but he gave himself no choice.

If the only way to make her see that was to tell her the truth, then that was what he had to do.

"A few years ago, I did something stupid and made a grave error in judgment. I got into some very serious trouble with the law. It was before I became a Christian, and I know God has forgiven me, but just because I'm right with God doesn't mean I'm right with the criminal justice system. I have a criminal record."

Her gasp stabbed him down to the depths of his soul, but it was nothing less than he deserved.

"Lots of people have criminal records. But I've known you almost all your life. You're not a criminal. You're a good man."

175

"I haven't killed anyone or done anything violent, but what I did was a felony."

"Wh—what did you do?"

Suddenly all the strength was zapped out of him. Trent sighed, leaned against the wall, and stared at the blank wall beside the door.

Anything was better than watching the shock and disappointment in Kim's face.

"It was before I became a Christian. I went to a party with some friends. There were drugs involved, and I knew it." He let out a short, humorless laugh. "I'm no angel now, and I certainly wasn't then. The cops busted the party. Russ had been charged before, and he said he would go to jail if he was caught again. He'd only just gotten married, and he didn't want his wife to know. When the cops came in, he jammed a bunch of stuff in my pockets, and I didn't know what it was. I should have known, because we'd all done a little cocaine at the party. But I really wasn't thinking clearly, for obvious reasons. He told me I'd get off with a slap on the wrist because it would be a first offense, so I agreed."

"It doesn't sound like that's what happened."

Memories of his arrest and the following court sessions flashed through his mind, as vivid as if they had happened yesterday. "We'd taken my car, and while the cops were inside arresting people, including me, they were also outside searching the cars. I don't know how it happened, but in addition to a rather large amount of cocaine that I had in my pockets, they found more in my car. I didn't know whose it was or how it got there. Of course they didn't believe me. I figure someone saw the cops coming and quickly put it in my lunch pail because I hadn't locked the car, and the lunch pail was sitting on the seat."

He almost laughed about the fact that instead of taking something *out* of an unlocked car, someone had put something worth a lot of money *into* his car. But it really wasn't funny at all. The end results would stay with him for the rest of his life.

"Naturally, my fingerprints were all over my lunch pail, and whoever did it was either pretty smart or very experienced. The only fingerprints on the lunch pail were mine. To make a long story short, things didn't go very well. I was a little stoned at the time, and I wasn't a stranger in the crowd where drugs were flowing freely. Compared to what could have happened, I guess Russ was right; but I ended up with a criminal record of having committed a felony of possession of narcotics, the amount exceeding what would be considered reasonable, as they say, for 'personal' use. I suppose I have to thank God that they didn't charge me for trafficking."

"Do you still see those people?"

"No. After that, they started avoiding me as much as I avoided them."

"Is that when you started to seek Jesus as your Savior?"

"No. I was actually pretty bitter about the whole thing. It was later, when you convinced me to start attending the college and career group at the church. Even though no one knew, no one asked about anything I'd done. Everyone simply accepted me as who I was for that day, and I knew God loved me the same way."

The unexpected touch of her other hand on his other arm made Trent flinch.

"I feel so awful for you."

"Don't. It's over now. I just have to live with all the restrictions. And not having to force anyone else into those same restrictions is part of it."

"I don't understand."

"You'll never know what it feels like having to say on job applications and credit requests that I have a felony on my record. I've been turned down for a lot, and people haven't even asked me about it. They just don't want to deal with me. That's the reason I'm upgrading at night school—so I can get into a good job that I can stay at for the rest of my life. It's been hard on my family, too. It's also put a lot of other restrictions on me. I can't even leave the country."

"Why not? They have to let you back in."

"It's not exactly that. I can certainly get a passport, so I can technically get *out*, but other countries that I would want to go to don't want to let a convicted felon *into* their country, especially since it's drug-related. I'm immediately under suspicion, whether I've done any-thing or not. I was an adult at the time, so it's part of my permanent record. It's just better to stay home."

"That's not such a bad thing."

Trent spun around so fast that both her hands dropped. Without thinking of what he was doing, he cupped Kim's face in his hands and stared intently at her, forcing her to understand his convictions.

"Maybe not for me personally; but when the day comes to get married, a couple should fly away on a great honeymoon to a far-off exotic land, and that wouldn't be possible with me. Being young and in love can make someone set aside goals and not feel restricted, but that won't last. I've always thought it would be great to travel someplace special with the one I love when the kids get old enough. But I won't be able to do that. I don't even want to think of what it would be like to tell a kid that their daddy had a felony conviction for possession of narcotics. Or what about wanting to travel after you retire? Would you be content to just stay home and look at the same four walls all your life?"

Kim's eyes widened, and she gulped. "When did we start talking about me?"

Trent had always thought about marrying Kim, from the day he took her to the hospital when they were both sixteen. Now, ten years later, he still thought about it—dreamed about it. But unlike the days of his youth, he now knew it could never happen. She deserved better than anything he had to offer.

He'd always thought about her. He'd also always thought about holding her close, staring into her eyes, just as he was doing now.

"Kim. . ." Her name tasted like honey as it rolled off his tongue.

She raised her hands and rested them on his waist.

Her soft touch was all it took. His eyes drifted shut, and he leaned down and kissed her, just like he'd always wanted to.

He expected her to flinch and push him away, and

he would have accepted that. But she didn't. Her hands slid up under his jacket and around to his back, pulling him in closer as she kissed him right back, which made everything better. Or worse. His heart pounded, and everything he'd held back for the last ten years surged forward. Kissing Kim was everything he'd ever dreamed of. Even with the bulk of his jacket between them, she was still soft and warm and a perfect fit.

He yanked himself away and dragged his hand over his face.

"That shouldn't have happened. I think I'd better leave."

Doing exactly as he said, without giving her a chance to respond, he turned, walked out quickly, and shut the door behind him.

Chapter 8

Kim watched Trent as he toed off his boots, then walked into the kitchen carrying a plastic shopping bag. "I didn't get much help at lunchtime today," he said over his shoulder as he turned down the hallway. "Only two of the ladies wanted to try making an angel, and neither of them got one even half done. What about you?"

Even though the angels' production was coming to a critical point, Kim didn't want to talk about their progress or lack thereof.

She wanted to talk about what had happened last night, not about what didn't happen at lunchtime.

For ten long years, she'd been wondering how she would feel if Trent held her in his arms and kissed her.

Reality far exceeded her fantasies. Until he abruptly

pulled away and bolted like a kid caught with his hand in the cookie jar.

All day long she'd been thinking about what he said. Actually, she'd thought of little else, including the angels.

She followed him into the kitchen. "I didn't have any real success either. Most everyone went shopping on their lunch break, so I was pretty much alone. Trent, what happened last night?"

At her question, he dropped a bag of beads on the floor. On impact, the bag burst and a hundred angel heads clattered and bounced and rolled helter-skelter. In an instant, Trent pushed the chair out of the way and lowered himself to his hands and knees and scrambled under the table to pick up the beads before they all escaped.

"I don't know," he mumbled, not raising his head. "Part of me wants to apologize; but part of me wants to do it again, and that's wrong."

Kim pulled a bowl out of the cupboard to put the beads into, lowered herself to her hands and knees, put the bowl between them, and also began to pick up the errant beads.

She spoke without actually looking at him. "As you can probably guess, I've been thinking a lot about last night, and you probably have been, too."

He grunted but otherwise didn't speak. Kim took it to be a confirmation of what she suspected.

"It's okay. I don't want to travel. I'm kind of afraid of heights anyway."

"Thanks for trying to make me feel better, but I'm really okay. I've dealt with it."

"It doesn't sound like it to me."

"I have. I've chosen to quit wallowing and get on with my life."

She wasn't so sure of that. Of course it was a positive step to attend night school, but she wasn't sure that was the answer. "But you're shutting yourself off from everything else—the stuff that's really important."

"I've chosen my path."

Kim had picked up all the beads in her area, but she remained on her hands and knees under the table with Trent, watching him as he gathered the last of what he could reach before moving and taking the bowl with him.

She didn't know if the travel restrictions were really so important to him. Many people with records traveled in foreign lands without incident. It was more likely that Trent had made his choices because of his other statement—one he'd only touched on briefly. He couldn't bear the thought that his future children would be disappointed in their father.

"You're forgiven by the only One who matters."

"I know that."

He shuffled away with the bowl to pick up the last of the beads that had rolled to the corner of the kitchen.

Kim's throat became tight. Instead of dwelling on past mistakes, she couldn't help loving the man who had lowered himself to the floor, literally, at least for the moment, to do something most men would never do. She knew most men didn't make beaded crafts, yet he'd swallowed his pride, even in front of his coworkers, to help when she needed it after making a mistake of her own.

She couldn't help loving him even more than she had before.

And now, after all these years of staying silent, he'd finally given her a sign that he felt something for her, too. Otherwise, he never would have kissed her, and especially not like he had.

It was time to stop waiting and do something. She could almost feel God pushing her to move forward.

She started to move in his direction, pushing her-self up in order to sit on the floor beside him, rather than to be so far away, hunched over under the table. "Trent, I was thinking. . . . Would you like to—*ow!*"

The clatter of movement of the beads, scissors, and paraphernalia from atop the table echoed, and a sudden sharp pain made a bright light flash before Kim's eyes. The world spun, and her head felt strangely warm.

"Kim! Are you okay?"

Her eyes stung. She blinked repeatedly, both to clear her vision and to steel herself from the pain at the top of her head.

When she pressed her fingers to the sore spot, her hair was warm and sticky.

Her head swam even more. "No. I think I hurt myself."

Red dripped onto the floor.

Her stomach churned. "Correction. I *know* I hurt myself."

Trent scrambled and was beside her in seconds. His face paled, and he glanced at her head, then bent down to look up at the underside of the kitchen table. "You cut your head open on the metal bracket." He crawled more quickly than she'd ever seen anyone move when not on their feet, grabbed the towel she had hanging on the oven door, wadded it up, and pressed it to the wound, slowly at first, then increasing in pressure.

"I'm going to assume that since you've been using this to dry the dishes you eat from that it's clean. How bad does it hurt?"

"Strangely, not that bad," she said, telling the truth. It had hurt on impact, but now the pain had lessened to a dull throb.

"Head wounds bleed a lot faster and with more blood loss than anywhere else on the human body. We have to take you to the clinic for some stitches."

Her head swam even more. "How bad is it?"

"I can't tell; I'm not a doctor. All I know is that you're bleeding. Put your arm on me, and I'll help you stand."

When she was steady enough, Trent walked her to the door and helped her slip her coat and boots on, making sure to keep constant pressure on her head. "If you're ready, let's go."

All the way to the clinic, she couldn't look at him. All she could think of was how history was repeating itself, this instance so like the one ten years ago when he drove her to the hospital after she broke her arm.

Again, over Trent.

She spoke while still looking blankly out the car window, keeping the soggy towel pressed firmly to her head. She did notice that this time he wasn't speeding quite as much as ten years ago. He'd also become a much better driver. "It's not your fault, you know."

"I don't know about that. I'm beginning to wonder if this is a sign or just bad luck. It seems we've been down this path before."

"The only one to blame here is me for being so clumsy."

"Are you usually clumsy?"

"Well. . .I—"

"I didn't think so. I'm so sorry, Kim. I don't know what to say."

"I said it's not you; it's me," she said, still not turning her head to look at him. "I'm the one who should be sorry. It's not fair for you to have to run to my rescue when I do something stupid."

"Like we agreed not so long ago, everyone makes mistakes. Here we are. Let's go in and get you all fixed up."

Chapter 9

K im yawned, then winced at the pull of the stitches on her scalp. She raised her hand, but before she could touch it, she heard Trent's voice.

"Don't touch it! You've got to let it heal properly and do your best to keep it clean."

"You sound like my mother," Kim grumbled.

"Sometimes having your mother around to remind you of things isn't necessarily a bad thing."

"I suppose not. I think that's just an expression, really."

"By the way, how are your parents? Where are they now?"

Kim sighed. She'd hoped her parents would come home for Christmas, but it wasn't going to happen.

"Last time I heard from them, they were in Florida and having a blast. I don't know how they can live like that."

"Lots of people travel around the country in a motor home after they retire."

"Yes, but for five years?"

"I bet they have some great stories to tell."

"That they do, and praise the Lord for e-mail and portable computers. How are your parents doing?"

"They love their apartment. They said selling me the house and moving to a smaller place was the best decision they ever made."

Kim yawned again, and she sank into the couch. "I don't know what I'm going to do. I can barely keep my eyes open. Those painkillers really wiped me out. I can barely see, never mind make more angels."

"If you want to go to sleep, I can still make some."

She closed her eyes and sighed. "You'll never be able to catch up with the number we missed doing tonight. And besides, even if you did, we still won't have enough. I guess it's time to just give up and admit I've failed."

"No. It's not over until it's over."

"The banquet is less than two days away. Even if we didn't sleep, if all we did was go to work and make angels, we still don't have time to make enough."

"It's time to call in reinforcements. I'll think of something."

"There's no one. I think we've both asked everyone we know."

Trent shook his head. "There's got to be someone, somewhere we didn't think of."

"If you can think of someone, I'll be grateful to you for the rest of my life."

Despite the worry and the overwhelming cloud of pending doom, Kim's eyes fluttered shut, and she couldn't stop them. "I'm so wiped out," she muttered as she snuggled into the couch. "Maybe these painkillers were just the right thing, because I don't even care anymore."

"You'll care tomorrow. But tomorrow is another day, and we both have to get up for work. Promise me you'll get yourself to bed safely, and I'll see myself out."

"Yeah. Sure."

Keeping the top of her head from touching anything, Kim buried her face into one of the cushions on the couch.

"Never mind. I'll see you tomorrow."

Instead of leaving, Trent stayed standing beside her. She heard beeping noises, then a gentle clunk on the coffee table.

"I've set the alarm on my wristwatch to wake you up in time to get ready for work in the morning. If you need me at any time, even in the middle of the night, just call. I can be here in under a minute."

"I know." And she knew he would.

Trent pulled the car to the side of the road and dialed Kim's office number on his cell phone.

"Trent? What took you so long? I've been waiting all day for you to call."

"I've been busy. I've got a solution—but we have to act fast."

"Pardon me?"

"I'm calling from my cell. Meet me at the craft store."

"What are you talking about?"

Trent barely kept from laughing. "I'm not going to tell you any more. It's a surprise."

"I don't like surprises."

"You're going to love this one. I'm already on the way. Bye."

He arrived at the craft store first. So as not to waste time, he found a parking spot and waited for Kim by the door.

He didn't wait long. In under three minutes, her car came whizzing into the parking lot. She'd obviously rushed, just as he'd requested, because when she found a spot and got out of the car, her coat wasn't fastened, and she was carrying her gloves and scarf instead of wearing them.

"This had better be good," she grumbled when she got within speaking range.

He tried to keep a straight face. "How's your head?"

She raised a shaky hand and brushed her fingertips along the wound. "It's very bruised feeling, but not bad. The worst thing is having to explain to everyone what happened. I wish they didn't have to shave so much of my hair."

"They really didn't shave that much; the nurse was very careful."

"I know. But it feels like a lot to me."

"It's not that bad. Really."

"Are you going to tell me what this is all about? I think you're stalling."

As usual, Trent was completely transparent. "Let's go in." He continued talking as they walked to the store entrance. "I called Josh, and he organized the youth group to have an emergency angel party. The kids are all out of school, so everyone managed to contact everyone else. In an hour, they're going to be meeting at the church, and we're having a late-night 'angel challenge,' the boys against the girls."

"Then what are we doing here? We've already got all the beads we need."

"I want to give prizes to the winning team, so I thought the most appropriate prize would be some kind of craft to make. I called the craft store to ask what kind of prize would be appropriate, and it seems the manager here has a nephew who has been going to our youth group. She's been so impressed by our youth group that she offered to donate a prize. So we're here to pick it up."

He was infinitely grateful that Kim had agreed to meet him there without question. Even though he'd been to the craft shop before, he didn't want to walk into such a place alone.

More than that, he needed to see her in private, to see how she was really doing, without an audience. Not that the craft store was all that private, but it was better than trying to find a minute alone in a building full of teens, whom they were supposed to be supervising.

The donated prize was a collection of small

Christmas decoration kits, suitable for both male and female crafters and easy enough to be an enjoyable project even for someone who wasn't very skilled at making crafts.

Trent tucked the bag under his arm and walked Kim to her car.

"We've got to hurry. We should be there before everyone else because we have to set up the piles for the kids to grab from. Then we each have to lead our groups; you lead the girls, and I'll lead the boys. I figure the challenge will be over when the beads are gone and the last angel is made."

"What if there are different numbers in both groups?"

He shrugged his shoulders. "Then we'll have to figure out some kind of handicap system before we start to make it a fair fight."

Kim rubbed her hands together. "I remember doing stuff like this when I was in youth group. It was a lot of fun."

"I hope so. We're going to have to fuel the competition somehow, rather than make it look like we're just desperate for numbers."

Kim grinned up at him, and he knew the flag had been dropped.

"I think when the boys lose, you should have to mow my grass all summer."

"I think when the girls lose, you'll be mowing my grass all summer."

"Not likely. Is this a challenge?"

Trent grinned. "You're on. May the best man win."

Kim stuck her nose in the air, snorted, and opened her car door.

"No. May the best woman win. See you there."

Chapter 10

"No, Tyler, you put the wire through like this."

Kim bit her bottom lip as she watched Trent out of the corner of her eye. She should have given the boys' group a bigger handicap.

But then, she really didn't like to mow the lawn.

She couldn't help smiling as she turned back to her own group. "Great work, Melissa. Would you like another piece of pizza?"

"I'm okay. These are fun to make. I think it's a great idea to give one to everybody at the banquet tomorrow night."

Kim smiled. With thirty-two teens diligently working as fast as they could, the angels would be finished in two hours. At the end, all they had to do was move the tables from the circles they now had set up into neat rows ready to be set for the banquet, and the youth group could do whatever they wanted to do for the rest of the evening.

Knowing that all the angels would now be done on time allowed Kim to not only relax but actually enjoy herself. With the challenge in place, both the boys' group and the girls' group had taken it as their personal mission to win.

While she didn't really want to mow Trent's lawn, Kim didn't care who won. The purpose was to finish the angels in time for the banquet, and now, since they were going to meet that goal, there wouldn't be any losers, only winners.

She lowered her current angel-in-progress when Trent walked toward her.

"I hope your group isn't cheating," he said loudly enough for everyone to hear.

"It's impossible to cheat, Trent. All the girls are following the instructions exactly, as are the boys."

All heads lowered as everyone returned their concentration to their projects.

"I don't know about that," he said as he came close enough for only Kim to hear what he was saying. "I heard whisperings that if we lose, a few of them are going to volunteer to take my place mowing your lawn once or twice, just so they can be with you for an afternoon. It sounds like someone has a crush on you."

"I don't think so," she whispered. "It sounds like they have accepted that the girls are going to win, and they're trying to make themselves feel better, as if they lost on purpose."

"The boys are talking about doing something else in a few months like this, except making the challenge more guy-related."

"That would probably be fun. And maybe a payback time would be good. I don't know how I'll ever be able to pay the group back for this."

"Don't worry about it. They're having fun. Can't you see how some of the boys have infiltrated the girls' group, pretending they need more help than they really do?"

Kim giggled. "Yes. I did notice that."

"After we're done, I was thinking that we should head over to the Midnight Madness sale at the mall. I want to buy a can of that fake spray-on snow and put some on the tree before we put the angels on. I think that would look good. Also, then the tree won't look so bare when we're taking the angels off to give them away."

"That's a great idea. One of the girls suggested

that I get a Christmas hat to wear tomorrow to cover my bald spot. I think I'm going to do that, and tonight sounds like a great time to buy a hat. There will probably be fewer people in the mall tonight than on Saturday."

"I agree." He jerked his head in the direction of the table they'd set up with the raw materials. "There aren't any more beads in the bins. We've come to the finish line."

Trent left her side and moved to the front of room. "We're down to the last ones, everybody!" he shouted. "Almost time for the countdown!"

All talking in the room stilled as the teens worked frantically to finish the angels they were working on. While the goal was to see which group could make more angels, they had agreed as part of the rules that when they were down to the last angels, whichever group finished first would get a bonus number for the number of angels the other group hadn't yet completed.

All the boys jumped to their feet. "We did it! We're done!"

A chorus of males grunting, "Whoo, whoo, whoo," filled the room.

"It doesn't matter!" Kim shouted to the girls' group. "We've done more. I know it."

They gathered around in two big circles.

"The boys did seventy-one," Trent said.

"Seventy-eight for the girls," replied Kim.

The girls cheered.

"Wait!" Trent called out. "We have to calculate the bonus points. The boys finished first."

Kim stood. "How many incomplete angels do we have on our side?"

Seven girls held up their angels-in-progress.

"That's seven points for the boys, so the winner is. . ."

The room fell completely silent.

"A tie," Kim croaked.

Both sides glared at each other.

Trent turned to Kim, lowering his voice so none of the teens would hear him. "I never considered the possibility of a tie."

Kim lowered her voice, also whispering. "Me neither. We needed an odd number of angels. It didn't even occur to me that the bonus points could even the score."

Silence loomed in the room.

"What about the prizes?" a male voice boomed from the back.

Trent retrieved the bag from under the table. "I

don't know. Let's see how many we've got so we can figure out a way to divide them up."

He pulled out a bundle of three plastic bags tied together with a large ribbon and a red bow.

"There's a note. It says, 'In this season there are no losers, only winners. Enjoy! God bless you all, Rochelle.' And look at this." Trent lowered the note and untied the bundle. "There are three bags, each with a dozen kits." He grinned. "We've got four more prizes than we have contestants. What a nice thing to do."

He gave one of the bags to Kim, and they handed out one to everyone. Immediately the teens began trading back and forth until everyone had exactly the kit they liked the best.

Kim also accepted a kit from Trent.

He winked at her. "I think we can each have one, too. After all, we were just as much in the contest as everyone else. I also think it would be nice to make something other than angels."

Kim grinned back. "I know what you mean. I think we should leave the last two for Stephanie and Pastor Mark."

Trent cleared his throat and raised his voice enough to be heard over all the chattering. "Okay, everyone! Let's get the tables back to where they belong, and then we'll start driving everyone home. Kim and I still have some shopping to do tonight."

"Shopping?" one of the boys piped up. "I still have a gift to buy. Can I come with you?"

"There's a big sale on tonight," a female voice joined in. "I'd like to go, too. I don't need a ride. My parents let me take the car. I just have to tell them I'm going to be late and where I'm going. They won't mind if I'm not alone."

"I've got a car, too," another of the boys called out.

Trent glanced around the room. "I can put five more in my car, and we can do three more in Kim's car. Josh can take four more. Who else brought their own car tonight?"

A few of the older youths raised their hands.

Kim forced herself to smile.

It was over. The angels were made, and she no longer had a reason for spending time alone with Trent. He'd made it more than clear that he had no desire for a relationship, especially with her.

Tonight was all she had left, and she wanted to spend the last of their time together alone with him. She wasn't ready to revert to the way things had been for the last ten years. One kiss had convinced her that things could be different. Trent just needed a little convincing to feel the same way. She only needed a little more time.

If they spent the remainder of this evening together, without any distractions other than shopping, she would have a better chance to convince him that his past record wasn't important—that they only had the future to look forward to. Regardless of what loomed in his past, a future together was better than a future apart.

Now that the pressure of making the angels was gone, this was the last time she would be with him, without the rest of the college and career group overseeing every move they made. At the mall they would be totally ignored no matter what they did, with everyone intent on their own business. Within the safe anonymity of the throng of holiday shoppers, Trent wouldn't be expecting her to pour out her heart until it was too late. Everything she ever needed to say to him she could say in the crowd at the mall. Being at the mall with him even forced them to stay together, regardless of his immediate reaction to what she said.

It was perfect. In the crowd of anonymous holiday shoppers, in effect, she would be holding him hostage.

But now it appeared the entire youth group was going to the Midnight Madness sale.

"Okay, everyone!" Trent called out. "We're ready. Let's go."

Chapter 11

"G ood-bye! Thanks for coming! And merry Christmas!"

Trent watched as Kim gave yet another couple from the church a big hug and sent them on their way.

The banquet had been a rousing success.

The drama group had put on a spectacular performance, and because of that, many people from the community who were not church members were staying behind to ask more questions.

The food was great, as Trent knew it would be. He couldn't remember the last time he ate so well, or so much.

And best of all, everyone loved the angel ornaments and were thrilled to be able to take one home.

As yet another family left, Trent scooted up the ladder, brought down another handful of angels, and gave them to Kim to give away.

Kim.

He watched her as she hugged someone else.

She wasn't hugging him.

Of course, that was by his own choosing.

Their time together at the mall played over and over again in his head. They hadn't been able to talk, at least not about anything too personal, but whenever they had been alone, as alone as one could be in the middle of a late-hours sale at the mall less than a week before Christmas, Kim had taken full advantage of every second.

He'd never allowed himself to consider her in a romantic way, at least not until recently, but when she had grabbed his hand, it was almost like coming home. Her hand was so small, yet with their fingers intertwined, the bond was so strong, all the pangs of loneliness left him so fast that he felt almost breathless. He could see the mischief twinkling in her eyes the second one of the teens caught them holding hands. He couldn't pull away without making it look like he was trying to hide.

She had him, and she knew it—except he hadn't

wanted to get away.

She said they could be happy together. Was it possible she was right? He'd never felt anyone support him, no matter what he did, like Kim.

He couldn't help it. He loved her. But he didn't know if that was enough.

Trent reached up to pull the last set of Christmas angels off the tree.

His heart pounded when his fingers brushed Kim's as she took the angels out of his hand and gave them to the last guests to leave the room.

He looked up. All the angels were gone. Every last one of them. The tree was bare.

As bare as his heart.

All that remained were the remnants of the fake snow he'd sprayed on, and some of that was falling off.

Despite what he had tried to do, the tree now looked ragged and exposed.

Trent could relate to the tree. He'd exposed his heart and all his ugliness to Kim, but she accepted him anyway.

Yet as they went their separate ways when they left the mall, something about her was different. Her good-bye wasn't in the usual mood of "see you later." It was different, as if for the first time she really meant good-bye.

He didn't know if he could be the man she deserved, but he sensed that if he let her go now, he would lose her forever.

Trent turned away from the tree to see that Kim had already moved away. She'd returned to the table where they'd sat together for the duration of the festivities, and she was now putting on her coat, getting ready to leave.

If he was going to do it, now was the time.

Trent gathered his courage and hurried to her side.

"Kim. Wait. Don't go."

She looked up at him, her eyes big and wide. And sad. So sad it tore at his heart.

He fumbled to find the little velvet bag he'd tucked inside his pocket.

"You were the only one who didn't get an angel tonight."

She smiled weakly, and her voice sounded far too timid. "It's okay. I've seen enough angels to do me for a while, I think."

He pulled the bag out of his pocket and pressed it into her palm.

"I knew you wouldn't get one, so I got you this instead."

"You didn't have to do this," she said without

looking inside the little pouch.

"But I wanted to. I saw it at the mall last night, and I bought it when you went into that store with Jeni. It's not much, but I thought you'd like it."

His heart pounded as she dumped his gift from the bag into her hand.

"It's a little angel. With a diamond on it. And it's a ring. . . ."

"Yes. But it's more than just a ring. It's a promise ring."

"A promise ring," she echoed hoarsely, in a voice little more than a whisper.

"Do you like it?" His heart pounded, waiting for her reply.

"Of course I like it. It's such a surprise; I don't know what to say. Why are you doing this?"

"When I bought it, I thought I'd give it to you for Christmas, but I can't wait that long. I had to give it to you now."

Her eyes became glassy, and she blinked a few times until they cleared. "I don't understand."

He reached forward and wrapped his hands around hers. "I've been thinking about what you said, and you were right. It's long past time for me to put the past aside and get on with my life. God has forgiven me, and that's all that matters. So I'm giving you this ring to start things off—to promise you that I'm going to try to be everything you need, first as a friend, and when the time is right, a husband."

Kim's eyes became glassy again, but this time, no amount of blinking stopped her tears from overflowing. "Are you proposing to me?"

Trent gave her a lopsided smile. "Not with just a little promise ring. But when the time is here, I promise you that I'll do it right." He paused, plucked the ring from her shaking fingers, and slipped it on her finger. It was a little big, but the saleswoman had promised they could size it after Christmas.

When the ring was in place, he rubbed his thumb over her finger, as if he could seal it in place. "I love you, Kim. I do want to marry you, but I don't want to rush things just because we've known each other nearly our whole lives. So take this ring as my promise that for once in my life, I'm going to do something right. I want to court you properly, take you out on dates and stuff, and then when the time is right, I want to propose the way it should happen. Maybe on a beach at sunset in the summertime. Something really romantic."

Kim pulled her hands away and rested them on his

waist. "I love you, too, and I don't have to do all that dating stuff. I'd marry you tomorrow, but if you want to wait awhile, I don't need a promise ring for that."

Trent reached down to her hand to touch the ring on her finger.

"Really?"

"Really." She smiled and raised herself up on her tiptoes, bringing her face close enough for him to kiss her. Except he didn't want to do that in the middle of the church, in front of the people who were now starting to clean up after the Christmas banquet.

She raised herself up even more. "But don't get me wrong. I still want the ring. It's gorgeous. And perfect."

Instead of kissing her lips like he wanted to, Trent grasped her hand, lifted it to his lips, and kissed the finger with the ring, his ring, on it. "Then I think I'd like a short engagement. Not that this is an engagement. I have a feeling the engagement will come soon. This is just a Christmas present."

Kim smiled, warming Trent from the inside out, like he'd never been warmed before.

"And with this Christmas present," she said softly, "this is the best Christmas ever."

Kim's Beaded Angel Ornament

Materials: Gold beading wire; 21 medium round
white pearl beads for body (suggested 5 mm);
1 large round white pearl bead for head (suggested 7 mm); 14 small white pearl beads for
arms (suggested 3 mm); 20 small gold beads
for halo (suggested 3 mm); 2½ inches (or
longer for large beads) ribbon-style lace (1½
inches wide) for wings; 6 inches thick gold
thread for hanger

Size: 2¼ inches tall when complete, not including hanger thread

Skill level: Easy

Time: About 20 minutes

INSTRUCTIONS

1. Cut a piece of beading wire about 18 inches long (if you use larger beads, you will need a longer piece of wire).

2. String 6 medium beads; push to the center.

3. Begin layering as follows: String 5 medium beads on one side of the wire; work opposite end of wire through newly added beads so that both strands of wire are going through the beads and coming out each end, layering the 5 beads above the 6 beads of the first row.

4. Continue to layer beads in the same manner with 1 less bead on each new row, until you have one bead at the top. Beads will form a triangle.

5. String 7 small beads for arms on one side.

6. Go around the 7th bead and reinsert the wire through the 6th bead and the remaining arm beads to "return" it, then through the single medium bead. You will end up with both wires sticking out the same side.

7. Repeat step 6 for the other arm using the

wire on that side.

8. In like manner, add the large white bead (head) by threading the wires through each side.

9. String all 20 gold beads on one wire, and thread it through the head to make the halo. Do not pull, but leave it loose.

10. String the other wire in like manner from the other side so that you have 2 wires going through the circle of halo beads and back out the sides of the head. Now pull the wires tight.

11. Thread both of the wires through the single medium bead (top of body triangle) as you did previously; pull wires to the back of the angel and set aside.

12. Pinch the center of the lace piece and tie one end of the gold thread around it. Do the same with the other end of the gold thread, making a large empty loop to be used to hang the angel.

13. Use the wires to fasten the wings to the back of the angel; clip the wires.

GAIL SATTLER

Gail Sattler lives on the West Coast with her husband, three sons, two dogs, five lizards, and count-less fish, many of which have names. Gail loves to write tales of romance that can be complete only with God in their center. She has had many books published by Barbour Publishing and its Heartsong Presents line. Gail was voted the Favorite Heartsong Presents Author for three years in a row and is now in the Heartsong Presents Author Hall of Fame. Visit Gail's Web page at www.gailsattler.com.

A Letter to Our Readers

Dear Readers:

In order that we might better contribute to your reading enjoyment, we would appreciate your taking a few minutes to respond to the following questions. When completed, please return to the following: Fiction Editor, Barbour Publishing, Inc., P.O. Box 719, Uhrichsville, OH 44683.

1. Did you enjoy reading *A Time for Angels*?
   □ Very much—I would like to see more books like this.
   □ Moderately—I would have enjoyed it more if _____
   _____
   _____

2. What influenced your decision to purchase this book?
   (Check those that apply.)
   □ Cover   □ Back cover copy   □ Title   □ Price
   □ Friends   □ Publicity   □ Other

3. Which story was your favorite?
   □ *Angel on the Doorstep*   □ *An Angel for Everyone*

4. Please check your age range:
   □ Under 18   □ 18–24   □ 25–34
   □ 35–45   □ 46–55   □ Over 55

5. How many hours per week do you read? _____

Name _____

Occupation _____

Address _____

City_____ State _____ Zip _____

E-mail_____

If you enjoyed

A Time for Angels

then read:

ONE CHRISTMAS ANGEL

*One Unique Christmas Angel, Handcrafted by a Child,
Brings Joy to Two Romances*

Strawberry Angel by Pamela Griffin
Angel Charm by Tamela Hancock Murray

If you enjoyed

A Time for Angels

then read:

patchwork CHRISTMAS

one woman's Legacy of hope
is bestowed upon two
struggling couples

Remnants of Faith by Renee DeMarco
Silver Lining by Colleen L. Reece

If you enjoyed

A Time for Angels

then read:

HOLIDAY HOPE

Love Has Much to Give
in Two Stories from the 1940s

Twice Loved by Wanda E. Brunstetter
Everlasting Song by DiAnn Mills